Helen Prothero Lewis, Helen Prothero Lewis

Hooks of Steel

Vol. I

Helen Prothero Lewis, Helen Prothero Lewis

Hooks of Steel
Vol. I

ISBN/EAN: 9783743418349

Manufactured in Europe, USA, Canada, Australia, Japa

Cover: Foto ©Andreas Hilbeck / pixelio.de

Manufactured and distributed by brebook publishing software (www.brebook.com)

Helen Prothero Lewis, Helen Prothero Lewis

Hooks of Steel

BY

HELEN PROTHERO-LEWIS

AUTHOR OF

"A LADY OF MY OWN," "HER HEART'S DESIRE," &C.

"The friends thou hast, and their adoption tried,
Grapple them to thy soul with Hooks of Steel."
—SHAKSPERE.

IN THREE VOLUMES—VOL. I

London 1894

HUTCHINSON & CO.

34 PATERNOSTER ROW

CONTENTS

BOOK I.

ORPHEUS WITH HIS LUTE.

BOOK II.

MY PRISON HOUSE.

BOOK I.

ORPHEUS WITH HIS LUTE.

HOOKS OF STEEL.

Book I.

CHAPTER I.

ORPHEUS is dead.   Dark as Erebus is his sleeping place on the Thracian hill.   No more do the savage beasts of the forest in listening to him forget their wildness, or the mountains bow their heads to hear him sing.

But his lute is in the heavens and makes sweet music amongst the stars.

Sometimes an echo of that music floats down to earth, but it is not given to all to hear.   The nightingales heard it as they wept round the grave of the dead musician, and ever since have sung of that heavenly strain.   Ever and anon a mortal hears it.   His eyes are divinely opened when he is gentle and pure in heart. The celestial song passes into his soul and remains there, and the strange power of Orpheus becomes his. Sweetness and harmony flow from him, and he can charm the wildest hearts by his gentle influence.

I knew one who had this power. He came into my life in its springtime, when the rose of youth was his and mine, and he touched my heart with his sweet and constant song of love, as Orpheus centuries ago touched the heart of the nymph Eurydice.

But alas! My wild nature proved stronger than his music. It gained dominion over me, my ears grew deaf to the sweet pleading—all the music was in vain. At length the singer wearied. Full of wounded love and sorrow, he took up his lute and wandered away to the mountains. The beautiful song died away in the far distance. I missed it when it ceased and looked round for the singer; but he was gone. Then, too late, I realized that without his music it was a dark and dreary world.

I purpose to tell you how I wrecked my fortune and my love. Wonder not, kind reader, that I lay bare my heart, and give to the world my story. It is meant as a warning note to all who shut their ears to the sweet music of beautiful souls: to all who trample on loving hearts and strike down kindly, outstretched hands: to all who, like the man with the muck rake, stoop down to grasp at bubbles unheeding of the love that offers them a crown. Nymph of to-day! Sister! Treading as I trod, heedlessly, along the path of life, if, as you read it comes over you that you too have been deaf to an Orpheus, repent ere the singer wearies and his song dies away in the distance.

It is a difficult task I have set myself. Very few people commit themselves actually to paper; put themselves unshrinkingly down in black and white. If the world wants the real man it flies to the biographer, feeling sure that by him every hidden weakness, every carefully kept secret, every sacred detail of the hearth and home will be unearthed and flaunted remorselessly in the eye of day. The biographer knows no reserve: to him nothing is consecrate, nothing is inviolable. The gratified world learns that the celebrated man changed his socks four times a week, and his shirt but twice; that he had a wart just below his collar, and a wife who drank. And it finds these details so interesting that a second edition of the book is called for immediately.

Very different is the autobiographer. He is loth, as a rule, to show you his real self. He would rather you did not know his wife drank, and he would be very likely not to mention the wart just below his collar.

I may fail sometimes in perfect openness, though I honestly wish to be open and true. But I will

not fail knowingly, nor deliberately hide aught
that can bear upon my story.

> Little shall I grace my cause,
> In speaking for myself. Yet, by your gracious patience,
> I will a round unvarnish'd tale deliver
> Of my whole course of love.

CHAPTER II.

I AM a girl, by name Rosamund Gwynne, and, as I write this, am a little over twenty-eight years of age. Perhaps some of my younger sisters may think that is rather old to be a "girl". Let them wait until they themselves are twenty-eight, possibly they will then think otherwise.

My birthplace was a sweet spot amidst the mountains of Wales. The name of our village .was "Llanfihangel-Aberbythich" which, being rendered into English means: "The-church-of the- angel -at -the -meeting -of -the -waters -which -is never-dry," and our house was called "Gwachel Foddi," which means: "Take-care-you-are-not-

8

drowned." Close to us was a hill called "Wedi-Boddi," which means "You-are-drowned", so we had both warning and illustration. No one ever was drowned because there was no water nearer than the reservoir, which was two miles off and carefully railed in. But the caution was kind, all the same. Ah me! I jest over these quaint old-time, misapplied names, but it is with tears in my eyes, for they touch my heart as the high sounding untranslatable names of English places never can.

I was an only child. My mother—no, I cannot write of my mother. In my heart there is a Holy of Holies. Between the kissing wings of love it lies. The mystery of death enwraps it, undying memory broods over it, there in that sacred place abides my mother.

Of my father I also, though for different reasons, find it difficult to write. He left when I was very young. He took the governess with him,

I was glad of that. Glad of it at the time, not understanding that it meant terrible grief to my mother. Later, I began to understand that there was a blank in that loved one's heart which not even I, her little daughter, could fill. She taught me, I was her companion by night and day, and there were times when I was an amazed hearer of grief too great to be restrained. These occasional glimpses into the blackness of desolation alone clouded the brightness of my childhood. Love and care surrounded my footsteps, tenderness was the atmosphere of my home. The gentle presence seems near me now as I write. Memories of those early days throng upon me, and more especially one in which I am lying in a small white bed by an open ivy-framed window, happy and drowsy in the summer dusk. By my side is the loved one holding my hand, so that my spirit may pass unfrightened into the world of sleep. And, past the window, skim those wonderful birds, the swifts, uttering the strange shrill cry that so speaks of summer. Unfading is this memory of my childhood.

When I was twelve years old my mother died. Dressed in crape, and weeping, bewildered and amazed by the sudden loss of my loved one, I was sent by my great-uncle, Lawrence Dillwyn, to school. A very cheap boarding-school at Exbourne, not at all the kind of place to which my mother would have sent her little daughter. But Lawrence Dillwyn was now my only living relative. When they wrote to inform him of my mother's death, he wrote back, directing that everything should be sold, and that I should be sent to this particular school, there to remain until he should be pleased to receive me in his house. There were none to gainsay him, and to this school I was accordingly sent. The parlour-maid took me there, a servant who had ever been a little stiff with me because I was trou-

blesome. But when she saw my helpless grief
and the meagreness of the home to which she
was about to consign me, a delicately nurtured
child, her heart melted within her, and after she
had bidden me farewell, she went out sobbing
through the doorway. With her, departed the last
trace of *home*.

O parents, uncles, and guardians, never send
your girl charges to a cheap boarding school! If
money be scarce let a reduced gentlewoman
come in and teach them every morning—there are
crowds of them who would be thankful to be so
employed—or educate them yourselves, but don't
send them to a cheap boarding school. Life being
short, time does not admit of my descanting at
full length on the evils of such institutions, but
I can at least speak of their effect upon myself.
In every way I degenerated; I was uneasily
conscious of it myself, even at that early age.
Especially did I degenerate in manner, tone of

thought, and style of conversation, as you will readily believe when you have followed me further. Children are essentially imitative: at home I had had a lovely model, and my old nurse was wont to observe that, with all her naughtiness, Miss Rosamund had the ways of a little lady. At school the atmosphere was very different. Miss Skinner, the head of the school, constantly spoke of herself as a lady, but she was apt to forget it when in a bad temper. Poor thing! she had a great deal to do. There were forty girls in the school, all boarders, and some of them very young, and she had only one assistant, a Miss Jones. According to the circular these two taught English in all its branches, French, German, and Italian acquired abroad, painting in water colours and oils, piano, violin, and guitar, calisthenics, needlework, dancing, and scientific cookery, and *when desired* Greek and Latin. Besides all this there was housekeeping, and marketing, and gardening, and account keeping, not to mention the dressing of small children, the nursing of sick ones, the care of wardrobes, the taking of daily walks, the interviewing of parents, and the punishment of culprits. Under such circumstances, it was scarcely to be expected that we should get much individual attention, nor were we inclined to quarrel with our governesses on that score. In fact, the less attention they gave us the better we were pleased.

I cannot say from what class my girl companions were taken. They were all absolutely unrefined, but then refinement belongs to no class. Since every Jack became a gentleman, there's many a gentle person made a Jack. I have known labourers with the manners and feelings of gentlemen, and I have known ladies indulge in conversation which might possibly be tabooed in the servants' hall. I have nothing to say against the poor girls. They suffered under the same disadvantages that I did. We all combined in hating Miss Skinner, and *faute de mieux* took Miss Jones for our model. She was a stout young woman, by no means dainty in her personal habits, and with a weakness for peppermint. But she had a pretty face, and a broad Dorsetshire accent which we admired immensely and took the greatest pains to acquire.

I will pass quickly over the first year of my school life. The first six months I cried a good deal and suffered from chronic and violent homesickness. I rebelled against my meals, sickened at sight of the dirty tablecloths, looked with aversion upon the six girls who shared my bedroom, and thought the smell of peppermint disgusting. By degrees all this wore off, and I managed to accommodate myself to my surroundings. Appetite returned, squeamishness left me, and I learned to enjoy my companions' society, and to converse, like them, with remarkable freedom and choiceness of expression. We were not "kept down" by overwork in our school. English in all its branches consisted of reading, writing, and arithmetic. Italian and German by tacit consent were never mentioned either by the governesses or their pupils, and profound silence was also maintained concerning the violin and guitar. French was of a most elementary description; no one seemed to get beyond "Have you the green coat of the carpenter's mother?" which came very early in the exercises. We discovered later that Miss Skinner and Miss Jones had never crossed the Channel, though they had acquired so many languages abroad, but the discovery made no disagreeable impression upon our minds. We also discovered that neither of our instructresses knew a word of Greek or Latin, but then, as Miss Jones observed, these dead languages were not taught *unless desired*, and as they never were desired, why should she know how to teach them!

The pianos received a great deal of attention; there were but two between the forty of us. Lessons on the instrument were few and far between; but we cared little for that, and enjoyed far more "practising" alone. The nature of that practising I leave to the imagination of the reader. Miss Jones used to look quite hot sometimes when both pianos were going at the same time, and observed once that two cats on a house-top were less trying to listen to, for they did get *pianissimo* sometimes.

One class came twice a week with unfailing regularity : the Literature-and-Sewing class. We mended Miss Skinner's stockings then, and our own clothes, and the house-linen, and we read aloud Shakspere by turns. It was soon ascertained that I mended very badly but read aloud uncommonly well, so my turn to read came very often. It was my great delight, my one perfect pleasure. I have loved Shakspere all my life ;

to me he has ever been the greatest wonder of
the world. Even in those far-off school-days,
when I was but a little lassie, too young to
understand half the great master said, I loved
him, and delighted in the grand majesty of his
utterances.

But alas! I confess it with shame, I put even
that master mind to base uses. I discovered by
degrees that nothing annoyed Miss Skinner more,
especially when she was already angry, than to
be talked to in Shaksperian language. Though
she presided over the Literature class, she was
never quite certain, when I became Shaksperian,
how much of what I said was Shakspere's, and
how much was my own, and this put her to a
great disadvantage. Afraid to betray her ignorance she seldom attempted a war of words with
me; either she let my remarks pass in angry
silence, or she bade me harshly hold my tongue.
My companions also occasionally found my pre-

dilection for Shakspere disturbing. I remember
well exasperating them one night beyond the
bounds of patience.

It was early in April, and I had been over a
year at the school without once leaving it. I
think I was rather a favourite with the girls.
True, I annoyed them constantly, but there was
a good deal of *esprit de corps* about me, and
they appreciated it. On this occasion we had
retired for the night, and I lay in bed side by
side with my six sleeping companions-of-the-bedchamber. Opposite the beds, against the wall,
were ranged seven small deal washhand-stands,
and between beds and stands was a bare space
of uncarpeted floor. To the right was the door,
to the left the window. The blind had been torn
down in a scuffle that morning, and the pale
moonlight crept in and lay upon the floor. 'Twas
very tempting, that space of uncarpeted floor,
I could not resist it. I rose teeming with Shak-

spere, and silently arrayed myself in my top sheet. This sheet had been overlooked at the last Literature class, and had a large hole in it, most convenient for the eyes. My next act was to stand near the window and give a blood-curdling groan. Instantly a row of white figures started up in the line of narrow beds.

"What is it?" exclaimed six voices affrightedly.

I began to strut up and down the moonlit floor declaiming again and again:

> "'I am thy father's spirit:
> Doom'd for a certain term to walk the night.'"

At first, though sleepy and half frightened, they laughed a little, but after a time they got tired of their father's spirit, and begged me to come to bed.

"Never!" I exclaimed. "I will make night hideous."

Then I gave some more blood-curdling groans and continued to strut up and down and wave myself about in the moonlight. In vain did my companions entreat me to stop or Miss Skinner would discover me. I was far too excited to heed their warnings.

"I cannot stop," I exclaimed, "I must do it to-morrow and to-morrow and to-morrow, I must creep in this petty pace from day to day like a wave o' th' sea, and murder him that first cries 'Hold, enough!'"

More wavings in the moonlight followed. The patience of my companions was exhausted. Isabel Sturgeon, the eldest, flung her slipper at me, and Amelia Macfarlane, the youngest of us all, tired, and bereft of hope, began to cry loudly.

"Rest, rest, perturbed spirit," I exclaimed, rushing desperately to the latter's bed, "I will go squeak and gibber in the Roman Streets. The hurly-burly's done."

It was too late. Miss Skinner had been awakened: we could hear her slip-shod feet approaching. The girls cowered back on their pillows, and the little one ceased her loud cries and whimpered softly. The next moment the door was flung open and our governess entered, her tall thin figure wrapped in a scant grey dressing-gown, beneath which appeared her lean and slippered feet. She held herself, as usual, very erect, and bore a lighted candle in her hand. The light caught her face, making her grey dishevelled locks shine, and her angry eyes gleam. Involuntarily as I looked at her I thought of the witches in Macbeth.

"Rosamund, what are you doing?" she asked sternly, in a voice shaking with rage.

My reputation was at stake. I felt I must not show craven fear before my companions, but be bold as a Nemean Lion if I wished to retain their admiration, so I answered boldly, peering at her through the hole in the sheet:

> "'Sleeping within my orchard, Madam,
> My custom always in the afternoon.'"

"Hold your tongue, you impertinent girl. Why have you been frightening Amelia, and how dare you tear holes in my sheets in the dead of night?"

The witch was beside herself with anger. Her grey tresses trembled round her face, so strong was the force of the passion that was shaking her.

Pleased with the excitement I was causing I answered coolly:

> "'Thou canst not say I did it: never shake
> Thy gory locks at me.'"

Miss Skinner grew crimson, and lost all command over herself. "How dare you?" she cried, and lifted her hand and struck me a sharp blow on the side of the head.

I staggered for a moment beneath it, but

recovered myself swiftly and stood erect, so full of
wild anger that for a moment I could not speak.

It must have been a funny picture; Miss
Skinner, tall and lean, in her scant grey dressing-
gown, facing me in my sheet, and the row of
girls sitting up in their narrow' beds, their eyes
fixed on us anxiously. Unfortunately I could
not see it, for my involuntary stagger had dis-
arranged the sheet, and the hole had slipped
away from my eyes. It was impossible to remain
in this position; so, after a moment of stunned
silence, I began to search for the hole, struggling
like a blind fury amongst the white folds. I
found it at last upon my chest, and seizing its
ragged edges, I tore the sheet asunder with
passionate violence and flung it round my feet
upon the floor.

"Rosamund!" exclaimed Miss Skinner, but the
Nemean lion was roused fully now, and could not
be checked with a word.

"Out, damned spot! out, I say!" exclaimed I vehemently, pointing at the same time to the door.

A chorus of low, frightened "Ohs!" came from the beds, and Miss Skinner turned quite white. I fully expected a second blow, but, to do the poor old creature justice, I really think, judging by the expression her face wore, that she already regretted the first, and now only longed to put an end to a scene that was imperilling her dignity. She looked at me helplessly for a moment, evidently quite nonplussed; then did the best thing she could have done under the circumstances, vacated the field. With all the dignity she could muster she walked slowly out of the room, and left me standing victorious in the midst of it, with my battle sheet around me. Of course it was quite evident that she wished me to understand I was too wicked for further notice, but I did not choose to take it so.

" She has gone, " I exclaimed hysterically, " gone,

as I commanded her." Then the Nemean lion broke down, and, weeping, I crept back to my bed.

"No one has ever struck me before," I sobbed. "Oh, my mother, my mother! I do want you so dreadfully. Am I never to go back to any home! Must I always stay here where everything is horrid, and dirty, and ugly, and no one loves me? Oh, my face hurts where she struck me, it hurts, it hurts!"

"She was a beast to hit you like that," said Isabel, sympathetically.

"Never mind," said Joanna Buckley, the girl who slept next but one to me. "Don't cry, it makes the eyes bad. The holidays are coming, and you're to go away for a bit then, aren't you, to stay with your great-uncle in his castle?"

"Yes," I answered, calming a little, and drying my eyes on the blanket. "He said I was to come at the end of this term for a fortnight, to show him how I was improving."

"Did you see his letter?" asked Joanna.

"No, it was not shown me," I answered.

"I did. I found it in Skinner's pocket when I was mending the seam of her afternoon gown, and I read it when she wasn't looking. Third class you're to travel, and a small black bag to save cabs. He doesn't seem very handsome about money. You don't even get a penny a week pocket-money like the rest of us."

"I don't care about money if I can get away from Skinner," I answered; and then, worn out by the conflicting emotions of the night, I suddenly dropped asleep.

O dearie me! I lived to regret my pranks upon that moonlit, uncarpeted floor. Bitter punishment awaited me, though it did not fall upon my defenceless head at once. I was, of course, made to mend the sheet, and being a little conscience-stricken I did it to the best of my ability, and made a very tidy job of it. Also, for the rest of the term I was banished from the Literature class, and Shakspere became a forbidden joy. Butter and pudding were also denied me at meal times, a very favourite form of punishment with Miss Skinner, but all these things were as trifles to one who, like myself, expected a speedy emancipation. An emancipation that would last a whole fortnight, 'twas delightful to think of. I drew vivid pictures of my uncle's castle, and of myself revelling there amidst unlimited butter and pudding, and endless editions of Shakspere.

" Breaking-up day " came at last. A few parents came in person to take their daughters away, saw the prizes given, and partook of tea in the drawing-room. Neither parents nor prizes came to me and I was glad when the ceremony was over. All discipline was cast aside then, and the girls rushed to their rooms to pack and get ready for their departure. I was rushing up with them, when suddenly I remembered I was to take a small black bag, so I went up to Miss Skinner and asked for one.

"A small black bag!" she said sternly, "what do you want with a small black bag?"

"To save cabs. It was in the letter; don't you remember?" I said incautiously.

"How do you know what was in that letter?" she asked sharply.

I made no answer. My thoughtlessness had led me into a scrape, but I did not mean to betray a companion-of-the-bedchamber.

"So you have been sneaking and reading letters behind my back, have you?" went on Skinner angrily. "Well, it is only of a piece with the rest of your conduct, though I did think you were above sneaking. I'll *give* you a letter to read this time, and you shall see how you like it. Here! Take this up to your room and read it, and you'll soon see you need no black bag. Black bag indeed! I never saw such a bold, wicked child."

I took the open letter she held out to me, and went up to my room. It was from my great-uncle, my mother's uncle, who was supposed to be very rich and who lived in a castle. He was a relation I had never seen. It was at his expense I was being fed, clothed, and educated. I had no reason to suppose his letter would be unkind, yet dull forebodings knocked at my heart as I sat down to read it. Around me were my companions packing joyously. Thus it ran, the fatal letter:—

" THE CASTLE,

" WILDACRE COMMON.

" MY DEAR ROSAMUND,

" In consequence of a letter just received from your kind instructress, Miss Skinner, describing your profane and destructive conduct, I must refuse to receive you in my Castle for the Easter vacation as had been arranged. I cannot entertain a child who uses bad language, and wantonly destroys property. I value my property: besides, I am really very poor. I have to pay the Lord of the Manor an annuity, and my Common, 5,000 acres in extent, has to be kept in a state of good preservation, which leaves great shortness of money for household expenditure. Under these circumstances, I think it will be best for you to remain where you are until you reach the age of seventeen, and are old enough to leave school altogether. I regret to postpone our meeting, but travelling, even third class, is expensive, and there would be nothing gained by your travelling to and fro. Please destroy no more sheets. I have had to send seven-and-sixpence to replace the one you have ruined.

"Believe me to remain,

"Your affectionate uncle,

"LAWRENCE DILLWYN."

"Thor's day."

CHAPTER III.

STUNNED and miserable I sat on the bed when I had finished reading the letter. Four years to a child is an eternity, and emancipation might have lain the other side the grave, for all the joy the thought of it brought to me. The girls soon saw there was something wrong and came crowding round me. I let Isabel take the letter from my limp hand and read it aloud to the others.

"Well!" she exclaimed when she had finished, "there's a stingy uncle! Bad language indeed! It's to save your railway fare he does this, it's as plain as a pikestaff. And there's nowhere he can board you so cheap as with Skinner. Oh,

I'd like to pay him out for this! Why, the man can't even spell: just look how he's spelt Thursday. Who ever saw it spelt 'Thor's day' before!"

"It's Skinner is at the bottom of it all," said Joanna indignantly. "She wrote him a pack of mean lies, I can see by this letter. That sheet has been no more replaced than I have. Rosamund made a very tidy job of it, and it's back on her bed now. *I'd* pay out Skinner if I could. It pays her to keep Rosamund four years straight on end, that's where it is."

Oh, yes! They were all very indignant and sympathetic, but that did me small good. Nothing they could say touched me or comforted me in the slightest. I sat on the edge of my bed motionless and dry-eyed, and felt as if I had been turned into stone. The girls resumed their packing at length, whispering to each other as they moved about the room, and every now and then casting a commiserating glance at me. When all was ready they put on their hats and jackets, and then they congregated in a corner, and there was much agitated whispering and a great searching of pockets and jingling of coppers. Then they approached me looking strangely sheepish, Isabel a little in advance.

" Rosamund," she said, "you know those shilling Shakspueres in the shop in the High Street, the ones you're always longing for when we walk past. Well, we subscribed two-pence each, that's a shilling, and you're to buy a Shakspere with it the first time you can slip out on the sly. And we'll be back in a fortnight, and when we come we'll pay out old Skinner for treating you so shamefully." So saying she placed the collection in my lap.

Dear girls! I can see you now, standing awkwardly before me in your cheap ill-fitting clothes, with your shabby trunks behind you.

Not one of you was pleasing to look at in reality, but to me at that moment you were transfigured, and appeared what all unselfish people are in a fair way to become, beautiful as angels in robes of light. I looked up at them, and the gate of my tears was opened. Taking up my black silk apron I covered my face with it, and sobbed amongst the coppers, and my heart went out to my companions-of-the-bedchamber. Their coppers were to them what pounds are to some people, each had given me a fortnight's pocket-money, just on the eve of their holiday which they had been saving up for. Poor dear girls! Never will I forget you. You all came from poor and sordid homes and went to lives of drudgery, but, please God, I shall have sweetened life for all of you before I die.

"Good-bye, Rosamund, don't cry, we'll be back soon," said Isabel, and then she kissed me. There were sympathetic tears in her own eyes as she

did so, and she sniffled a good deal into her
pocket-handkerchief. It was a singularly dirty
handkerchief, but I could have had the loan of
it if I had liked, or of anything else that was
hers, so let no one think the worse of the owner.
Ten minutes later they had gone, and I was alone
in the room.

There I and Sorrow sat. I tried to stop crying
but could not, so bitter a sense of home-sickness
and desolation was upon me. At length I went
to the window, threw it open, and thrust my
feverish convulsed face out into the cold air. It
was a very wet world I looked out upon. The
earth was soaked with rain, and the trees waved
and dripped in the garden of our neighbour. A
shower had just passed, and dark, low hanging
clouds showed that another was imminent. As
I leaned out, I longed, with a longing that was
absolute pain, for my mother-home in Wales.
It is curious, but to this day an interval between

two showers gives me a feeling of home-sickness, and makes me long for Wales. I think it is the effect of early associations, which have a stronger influence on the mind than aught in life besides. Whispers from the vanished past mingle with the breath of the fresh rain-laden wind; vague memories of childish days haunt the gleaming puddles, the dripping hedges, the diamond-spangled grass; dear and familiar is the grey far-off line of the advancing rain, which comes like a messenger from over the mountains. No one who is not familiar with them can imagine the delight and sense of refreshment given by constant showers. The earth is so refreshed and rejoicing. Its breath is like a song of praise as it rises to the kindly, down-sweeping clouds. Like sweetest incense is the fresh scent of the grass and flowers; like loveliest jewels are the hanging raindrops; calm and sweet is the line of yellow on the horizon, beyond the hills. It may be difficult to believe, but a true Welshwoman loves the damp, rejoices in a shower, and exults in a storm.

My tears continued to fall as I leaned from my window and watched the sweeping clouds, but after a little time, chancing to look down to the left, I saw a sight which suddenly checked them. A fine large house stood next to ours, half hidden by trees, through which its many windows glittered on sunny days like great diamonds. It was surrounded by a beautiful garden which, on our side, sloped down to a low wall which was also the boundary line of Skinner's little strip of flower-beds. These flower-beds lay beneath my window and now, as I looked down upon them, I saw, leaning against the further side of the boundary wall, a tall boy watching me. Nay, perhaps he was rather too old to be called a boy, we'll call him a young gentleman.

I had never seen him before, but at the first glance I could perceive that he was superior —

superior, at any rate, to us of the boarding-school.
He wore a knickerbocker suit of pale grey, very
good clothes indeed, and he looked altogether the
sort of boy to have plenty of pocket-money. His
attitude too, was superior, as he leaned with careless
grace against the wall, and there was something
proud in the way he held his head. He had a
bright kind face, nevertheless my first feeling at
sight of him was one of anger. His superiority
annoyed me, and it mortified me excessively that
he should have seen me cry.

"Go away, you horrid mongrel," I called out
to him. "Be somewhat scanter of your maiden
presence."

The young gentleman started. Then he straight-
ened himself, raised his eyebrows, and gazed
at me with an expression of unbounded wonder.
But he did not go away.

I proceeded to make the most horrible grimaces,
twisting my features into every contortion possible

to the human face. At first my intention was only to make his stay unpleasant, but as I went on I forgot my home-sickness, and, absorbed in my efforts, began to enjoy myself thoroughly. Presently it struck me as curious that the young gentleman never once smiled or looked amused. He simply resumed his superior attitude, and, with a critical expression upon his face, continued to watch me. A fierce determination to make him smile came over me. I left the window; tossed my hair into a yellow heap at the top of my head, stuck my comb bolt upright in it, soaped my nose well, then presented myself again at the window. To my great mortification, after the first glance the young gentleman took off his hat, made me a little bow, expressive of thanks and farewell, and walked away. My cheeks burned with shame as I watched him, and I began to regret I had gone so far. A line from Shakspere haunted me unpleasantly as

I washed the soap off my nose, and combed my tangled locks down again:

"Be thou familiar but by no means vulgar."

"Yes," I said to myself, regretfully, "I have been vulgar; next time I will be familiar, nothing more."

But the young gentleman had had enough of me and did not come again to the wall, though I watched for him continually. I had no chance of being either vulgar or familiar, which was a great blow to me. Oh, how long the days were! To do Miss Skinner justice she did not make my holiday more disagreeable to me than was inevitable. She gave me no tasks, took me out with her when she went calling, and supplied me with plenty of literature of a harmless description, Shakspere excluded. But she was a grim companion for a child, and I had no other the better part of the time. Of course I was never allowed

to go out alone, and though I watched carefully,
several days elapsed before I was able to slip
out and invest in the longed-for volume of Shakspere.   At length an opportunity presented itself
in this wise.

Miss Skinner had been asked out for the day,
and I was not invited to accompany her.   She
decided to go, and to leave me in charge of Mary
the housemaid.   At eleven o'clock she came down
ready to start.   She had on her best black silk
dress and jet-trimmed mantle, and I noticed that
she had smartened up her old black straw bonnet
with a red feather, and had red mittens on over
her old black kid gloves.

"Now, Rosamund," she said, taking up her
reticule and hanging it over her arm, "be a good
girl and don't give Mary trouble whilst I am
away.   You can help her to weed the walks
amongst the flower-beds in the afternoon, the fresh
air will do you good.   I have placed your dinner

ready for you in the schoolroom ; a nice slice of
cold bacon and some lettuce, and bread pudding
to follow. Give her some tea when you have
yours, Mary, and there's some dry toast left from
my breakfast she can have. I shall not be home
before seven. I think that is all there is to think
of : good-bye, Rosamund."

She went. The cook was away on a holiday,
Mary and I were alone. I looked at Mary: she
was a plump, good-humoured, bonnie lass, but she
stood between Shakspere and me. I felt it would
be a discredit to myself to allow her to remain
in such a position. Miss Skinner might be too
much for me, but Mary--oh, absurd !

Now Mary had a lover, a young man who
worked in a timber yard. Miss Skinner did not
allow followers, but maids care little for such
prohibitions.

"Mary," I said, "would you like to see your
young man to-day ? "

Mary grinned.

"Well," I said, "let us take a walk in the High Street, and I'll take a look at the books whilst you slip round to the timber yard."

"I daren't," said Mary, "the timber yard's a full mile away, and it's as much as my place is worth to leave the house and no one to answer the door."

"Oh, well," I said, "I'll stay and answer the door, that will be no trouble. It's a pity you shouldn't see Sam. You needn't stop long, and you could ask him to tea, Miss Skinner won't be home until seven."

Mary looked tempted. She was fully aware the whole school took a deep interest in her love affair, so was not surprised at my manœuvring to help her. After a little demur she yielded to the temptation, and left the house, begging me to keep a sharp eye on the door.

"And you won't split on me, Miss, will you?" she said, as she departed.

"Of course not!" I answered indignantly, "you wouldn't split on me and get me into trouble, would you?"

"Never, whatever you did, Miss," she answered warmly.

This was satisfactory, most satisfactory. I watched her until she was out of sight, then I packed up the cold bacon in a lettuce leaf and put it in my pocket. Next I tore the fly leaf out of a school book, wrote on it:

"Out for the day. Don't tell."

and tied it to the knocker of the front door with some black wool out of Miss Skinner's work-basket. These simple preparations completed I put on my hat and jacket, walked out of the house, and slammed the door behind me. I was free! O glorious Liberty! Free until seven o'clock. Quick as my feet would bear me I sped to the High Street, nor paused until I reached the bookseller's shop. Another moment and twelve coppers lay on the counter and the long-coveted Shakspere was in my hands. A bulky, badly-printed volume, but mine own. On, on, to the sea and there I seated myself on the shingly beach and fell like a hungry hawk upon the precious volume.

I read through the whole of "Hamlet" and the whole of "Macbeth" without stopping. Then, a little weary, I desisted and resolved to eat some cold bacon before proceeding to "Romeo and Juliet." I drew it forth : it looked perfectly horrible ! I had been sitting upon it for two hours, so this was scarcely surprising, but 'twas very disappointing. Not a morsel had passed my lips since the meagre breakfast at eight o'clock, the sharp sea air had made me exceedingly hungry, and here was my dinner spoilt, absolutely uneatable ! I flung it from me far as strength permitted, and soon had the pleasure of seeing a four-legged snapper-up of unconsidered trifles enjoying my dinner. Then I returned to my Shakspere, but somehow the god of my idolatry had no longer any power over me. My mind was cloyed, my body famished, and the depression which accompanies hunger began to steal over me. I laid my book on my lap and looked round dejectedly. In front of me lay the sea, blue, tossing, and restless, with white sails scudding away in the distance like wandering spirits seeking some lost happiness beyond the wave. Behind me, on the path, people were walking and talking together, and on the beach on either side of me were groups of happy children playing merrily together in the spring sunshine.

Soon a lady passed me, holding by the hand a beautifully dressed little girl, whose fair hair floated far down her back like mine. Something in their look as they passed together seemed to awake a sleeping memory. They stared at me a good deal as they passed, and I became suddenly conscious that my black frock was very shabby and my shoes much the worse for wear.

"That little girl looks very lonely," I heard the lady say as she passed, and then in a very gentle manner she added, looking down upon her little daughter, "Don't drag, dear."

A sharp pain darted through my heart. Was it in another world that I, beautifully dressed like that little girl, used to walk in the sunshine clinging confidently to a loved one's hand, and a gentle voice used to say to me: "Don't drag, dear."

Suddenly it came over me that I was very lonely, terribly lonely. So overpowering was the feeling that it was like physical pain. I hung down my head and hot tears dropped upon my lap. Someone drew near as I sat thus, I heard the heavy footfall scrunching the shingle, and looking up I saw before me the young gentleman of the wall. He had caught me again, like Niobe, all tears! I felt furious with myself, and sitting bolt upright tried to took as if I had never shed a tear in my life. But the young gentleman was too sharp for that. He halted in front of me, and said in a quiet composed voice:

"What is the matter, little girl?"

"Private," I answered grimly.

He tried again. "What is your name?" he asked gently.

"Born without one;" I said in the same tone.

I had once replied thus to a new girl's question as to my name, and the answer had been thought very witty in our school. I fully hoped the young gentleman would think it witty also, but to my discomfiture, my answer drove him away a second time. He lifted his hat and was gone.

"Be thou familiar but by no means vulgar."

I began to realize that I had overstepped the

bounds of familiarity. How soon, how pitiably soon had I forgotten the great master's teaching! If I had not replied so rudely the young gentleman might have stayed, I might have found a friend. Alas, poor Yorick! Where be your gibes now? Your flashes of merriment that were wont to set the table on a roar? They stand confessed as pure vulgarity.

The young gentleman walked steadily on for some time, then he turned and came back again towards the pier. He passed close in front of me, but this time he did not even glance my way. A sudden impulse seized me, and as he was walking on I called out desperately:

"My name is Rosamund."

He wheeled round instantly, and came and stood in front of me, smiling pleasantly.

"And a very pretty name it is," he said, "Rosamund, fair Rosamund. It suits you. But where is Queen Eleanor?"

History was not a strong point in our school. I had not the least idea what he meant by such a question, but I did not wish to betray ignorance, so I answered promptly:

"Gone home for the holidays."

"And why have you not gone home too?" he asked, seating himself by my side with a quick look at my shilling Shakspere open at "Romeo and Juliet," and blotted with tears.

"I have no home, and my great-uncle would not have me."

"Why would he not have you?"

"Because Miss Skinner wrote and told him I used bad language and wantonly destroyed property, and his property is 5,000 acres in extent, so he doesn't want it destroyed."

"But did you do what Miss Skinner accused you of?"

"I was only acting Shakspere, and I tore an old sheet, but I mended it afterwards. And now I

am not to leave the boarding school for four
years, not until I am seventeen! And all the
others go home every holidays. That is why I
was crying on the breaking-up day. And to-day
I cried because I felt so lonely after that little
girl passed with her mother. But I don't cry as
a rule."

"You cried very often when you first came to
school ?"

"How do you know ?" I asked, too surprised
to be angry.

"I saw you in church," he said. "I sit a long
way off, but I have good eyesight, quite good
enough to distinguish a little figure in black, that
wept every Sunday all through the service."

"It was the hymns," I said, getting very red;
"hymns always make me cry."

I was speaking the truth. Like Jessica, I am
never merry when I hear sweet music. To this
day church music gives me pain and fills me

with a sense of something wanting, which may be found the other side the grave, but not here.

"Why did you not laugh the other day?" I proceeded, wishing to change the conversation.

"Because," he answered, "I was sorry to see anyone made beautiful by nature distort herself into ugliness."

"Am I made beautiful by nature?" I asked.

"Yes, I think so," he said, looking at me meditatively. "You have what I am particularly fond of, blue eyes and golden hair."

I smiled broadly, and began to think I should like my new acquaintance.

"And you look a little lady," he went on, "therefore it is doubly a pity you should behave like a street Arab."

This remark also pleased me, it was so nice to hear that, notwithstanding my shabby clothes, I looked like a little lady.

"I like you," I said, "we'll be familiar. Now

tell me, where do you live and what is your name ?"

"I have just come to live next door to you," he said, "and my name is Felix, Felix Gray."

"Felix. You have a pretty name too. I like Felix immensely. Are you Welsh? I do hope you are Welsh, because I am. My other name is Gwynne, quite a Welsh name."

"Yes, I am Welsh on my mother's side, she was a Vaughan-Price, but my father was English. Don't catechise me further now, I want to know more about you, poor forlorn little maiden. Have you no mother?"

"No," I said in a low voice, the ready tears leaping to my eyes again.

"Poor child! And no father?"

"Oh, yes! I have a sort of father."

"Why don't you go to him in the holidays ?"

"Never," I answered fiercely.

"Surely you would rather be with your father

than at school! At least there would be no Miss
Skinner to worry you."

"Oh, there would be someone just as bad.
He's got my old governess."

"What do you mean?" asked Felix, looking
puzzled.

"Oh, I must not mention her name, it must never
be mentioned. But he took her away when we
lived at home, years and years ago, and he never
came back. No one knows where he is now."

"Poor child!" said Felix again. He had a
very nice voice, and something in it, perhaps the
ring of true sympathy unmistakable even to a
child's ears, touched my heart and turned it to
him. Drawing closer to him I continued in a
very low tone.

"The other one you asked after used to cry a
great deal because he never came back. I used
to hear her crying in the night—the loved one,
crying! And I knew why when I grew older,

and I *hated* him! She cried because she was
lonely and had only her one little girl. And she
cried more and more before she died. I am glad
now she has gone to heaven and cannot cry any
more. But I want her! oh, I want her, Felix!"

Then I burst into an anguish of tears. Felix
did not speak, he did not even look at me, but
he took my hand and clasped it gently in his
own until the storm of grief was over. Something
in his clasp gave me a curious, long-lost sense
of protection, and eased my sense of loneliness
and homesickness strangely. Soon my tears
ceased to fall. I looked down at the hand that
clasped mine. A nice cool hand. The hand of a
gentleman, with a crested gold ring on the third
finger, and gold studs in the spotless cuff. The
hand of a friend, there was real tenderness in its
clasp.

We sat quiet for a moment or two, he and I,
and I felt unusually happy. No longer did I

envy the children playing on the sands in the sunshine, or the gay people talking on the path behind me. I had a friend of my own now. The white sails in the distance were no longer lost spirits searching for happiness beyond the wave; they were beautiful sea-angels racing about and playing with each other, and the blue transparent ocean was the home of joy.

The ocean has rolled between Felix and me since then. Long, long years have parted us. But never once since that moment by the shore just described, have I doubted Felix's kind and faithful heart. I know that from the first moment we met, he has been constant as the Northern Star. But I—alas! in writing of myself I write,

> "—of one whose hand,
> Like the base Indian, threw a pearl away
> Richer than all his tribe."

CHAPTER IV.

FELIX and I sat hand in hand and happy, but time sped on and I had not dined. The pangs of hunger began to reassert themselves, and became unbearable. Longingly my thoughts turned to the bread pudding I had left behind me on the schoolroom table.

"I don't think I can sit still much longer," I observed pathetically, "I am so hungry I have got quite an empty pain."

"Hungry! Have you had no dinner?" asked Felix, turning quickly upon me.

"No," I replied. "I have had nothing since breakfast, and there wasn't much bread and butter then. There was some nice cold bacon for my dinner, but I sat upon it until it ran into the lettuce."

"What a shame!" exclaimed Felix, starting up and pulling me to my feet so abruptly that I looked at him half offended. "Come with me at once," he went on, drawing me along without heeding my injured glance. "You shall have some food before you go back to that precious Miss Skinner, or my name's not Felix."

Nothing loth, I let him draw me on, though he walked so fast I had much ado to keep up with him. He led me to the High Street, and presently stopped at a confectioner's shop, the windows of which had dazzled my eyes many a hungry day.

"We'll see what we can get here," he said, to my delight, and then took me in, and I was given a seat on a chair before a round marble table.

"Now, what will you take?" asked Felix.

My eyes roved to some delightful looking ham sandwiches in a glass jar.

"I should like one of those, please, if they are not too expensive" I said humbly, feeling almost awed by my good fortune.

"Too expensive, nonsense!" said Felix, "and now what would you like to drink : lemonade, milk, coffee?"

"Oh, lemonade, please, I used to be so fond of lemonade. But, Felix, are you sure you have enough pocket-money to pay, because I have none."

"Don't trouble your poor little head about the paying, leave that to me, and do enjoy yourself, Rosamund."

I did enjoy myself. I eat all the delicious sandwiches, and then I had some jelly and biscuits, and then I had more jelly and a Bath bun, and I drank two bottles of lemonade, and ate sweets until I could eat no more, and was given a huge packet to put in my pocket to take home. Felix paid for it all, and tossed down shillings as if they were coppers. I thought he looked such a gentleman, and told him so when he came out. But he only laughed and would not let me thank him.

As we walked home I explained to him how I had come by my Shakspere and told him how deeply I loved it. He listened with much interest. That was ever one of Felix's pleasant characteristics. He always listened as if he were interested, and I do like that in a person. So many men nowadays only care to hear themselves talk.

All too soon we reached Miss Skinner's door. I guessed Mary had returned because the notice was gone from the knocker, so I knocked boldly. My knock was promptly answered by Mary herself. She looked flushed and anxious, and her hair was much dishevelled, an invariable sign that the disallowed follower was haunting Miss Skinner's back premises. A capital idea occurred to me. Sam was evidently having tea with Mary, why should not Felix have tea with me?

"You naughty girl, Miss Ros'mund, for shame to you!" burst forth Mary impetuously; then she stopped abruptly, for her eyes fell upon my companion.

"Mr. Gray, a friend of mine," I said, waving my Shakspere carelessly in his direction. "A gentleman of princely parentage and stuffed with honourable parts"—   .

"O lor'! You're always on with your Shakspere," said Mary angrily. "Excuse me, Sir, but Miss Ros'mund has no business"—

"Mr. Gray has come to tea, *as you have Sam with you in the kitchen,*" I said very pointedly, staring fixedly at Mary as I made the remark.

"Oh, no, Rosamund, I must go home to dinner," put in Felix, with a great show of resolution.

I kept my eye on Mary and she understood that eye. I was small but determined, and she felt she must accept the situation if she did not wish to risk hers.

"Please walk in, Sir," she said, turning affably to Felix, "Miss Skinner won't be home for a couple of hours yet."

"Do," I said, looking at him pleadingly, "do, do, dear Felix. It is so lonely in that bare schoolroom by myself."

Felix hesitated. Then again he refused, but I only entreated him the more and, taking his hand, strove to draw him in. At last he yielded. I know he felt he ought not to come in, but from first to last that dear kind heart could refuse me nothing. He consented to come in for ten minutes! I led him to the schoolroom, a square uncarpeted room with three long deal tables flanked by benches ranged along it side by side, and maps on the yellow-painted walls. There

was the bread pudding still awaiting me, but how
I despised it now!

"Come and sit here, Felix," I said, pushing the
cold pudding aside and sitting down to the table.
"Come and sit by me on this bench. Oh, this is
nice, this is real holidays! If only Skinner could
be drowned that they might last for ever."

The ten minutes lengthened into twenty, and
still Felix stayed and listened whilst I poured
into his bent and kindly ear the story of my little
life, made a little obscure perhaps by perpetual
digressions into Shaksperian language, but evidently interesting to Felix. And then up came
brave Mary, bearing on a tray two cups of tea and,
oh, good creature! two fresh hot slices of toast. She
placed the tray on the table before us, and with joy I
prepared to play hostess for the first time in my life
when, oh, horrible! three quick raps on the knocker
burst upon my frightened ears. I gave a jump,
for 'twas the well-known knock of Skinner.

"The missis!" exclaimed Mary, turning pale.
"Oh, Mr. Gray, it's as much as my place is worth
for you to be caught here with Miss Ros'mund,
and me allowing it."

Felix glanced at the window.

"No," I said, "you can't escape that way. It's
nailed down because we used to climb out. But
you must hide somewhere; you don't know Skinner when she is angry. She hit me last time."

"Hit you!" exclaimed Felix indignantly, "fancy
hitting a delicate little creature like you! Where
shall I hide, Rosamund? I hate getting you and
Mary into trouble."

"The cupboard!" cried Mary with sudden
inspiration, and then she flung open the door of
a large cupboard in the wall behind us. Inside
was a row of pegs from which usually depended
our walking cloaks and hats, but now, luckily,
though dark and dirty 'twas empty save for my
mackintosh. Felix hesitated; it evidently went

against the grain to hide in a cupboard. Three raps, louder and angrier than the first, again resounded through the house.

"Oh, dear!" I cried, "she's getting furious, she's getting more inexorable far than empty tigers, whatever shall we do?"

"For your sake then, Rosamund," said Felix, and bolted into the cupboard. I flung the Shakspere in after him, and the next instant the lock was turned upon him and Mary was answering the door.

"I'm so sorry, Ma'am, you should have been kept waiting," I heard her saying in the passage, "but I was just carrying up some tea for Miss Ros'mund and myself to the schoolroom, thinking 'twould be lonely for her to have it by herself."

"Oh, well, lock the front door, no one will be going out again," replied my instructress in her loud harsh voice, "and just come in here and take off my goloshes!"

She walked into her private sanctum, which was just opposite the schoolroom, as she spoke. Felix gave a low groan.

"Hush!" I said in a whisper through the keyhole; "she's still near."

"But she's cutting off all escape," he whispered back, "and what shall I say if she comes to this cupboard and finds me here?"

'Twas a difficult question, but the student of Shakspere need never be long at a loss. "Cry, 'Havock!'" I whispered energetically through the keyhole, "cry 'Havock,' and let slip the dogs of war."

Then a still better idea occurred to me. I drew forth the key of the cupboard and put it in my pocket. The next instant Miss Skinner entered.

"Good evening, Rosamund," she said, putting her reticule down upon the table, and proceeding to remove her red mittens and black kid gloves. "I am glad to hear from Mary that you have been a good girl and have given her no trouble. Did you enjoy your dinner? I see you have not eaten much of the pudding."

"Yes, Miss Skinner, I enjoyed it very much, thank you," I answered, in my very best school-room manner.

"And did you weed the walks?" she asked next, removing her jet-trimmed mantle, and hanging it over the back of a chair.

"Yes, Miss Skinner, but the weeds spring up· again as fast as you pick them."

"That is a slight exaggeration, Rosamund," she said, smoothing her hair under her bonnet as she sat down to the table. "Weeds certainly grow very quickly, but not quite so immediately as you describe. You should try to be more accurate. I shall inspect your work to-morrow morning.— As you see, Mary, I have returned earlier than I expected, but my friend had such a headache I felt I really ought to leave. You had better have your tea downstairs now and I will have mine with Miss Rosamund. I see you have warmed up the toast, so we shall do nicely."

Mary scuttled away looking much relieved, and I was left to have tea with Miss Skinner, Felix close behind us in the cupboard. I don't think I have ever seen Miss Skinner so good-tempered or so garrulous as she was on this occasion. The day's outing had done her good, and she discoursed with unwonted affability as she drank her tea.

"I have been hearing about our new neighbours," she said presently, "the people who have taken the large house with the beautiful garden next door. Miss Robinson's cook knows the housemaid there intimately, so Miss Robinson was in a position to give me a great deal of information about them. The family consists of Mrs. Vaughan-Price, a very rich old lady, and her grandson Felix Gray, the son of her only daughter who died some years ago. The grand-mother's got a shocking temper, no servants stay there long. Comes down in black silk and real lace, and most beautiful diamond rings. A fresh joint every day, and a good table kept even in the servants' hall. They keep two gardeners. Oh dear! how I wish I could have a few spare roots from that lovely garden. My poor little beds look sadly empty. They may say what they like, but things aren't equally divided in this world. I toil to raise a few geraniums, just for the love of them. That old lady has acres of flowers, and doesn't go once a week to look at them. Pass the toast, my dear."

I passed the toast, and hoped no more would be said about the family life of the gentleman in the cupboard. For a moment Skinner was silent and scrunched her toast, then she began again:—

"They say the young man is quite dependent on his grandmother. His father died almost a pauper. But he's to be his grandmother's heir on one condition,—that he marries his cousin, Angharad Vaughan-Price, the daughter of the old lady's only son, and the heiress to Cwmcoch Hall, the Vaughan-Prices' family place in North Wales."

Here her speech was interrupted by a scuffling noise in the cupboard. I knew 'twas Felix making an impatient movement, and the frightened blood rushed to my cheeks. Was he angered by this news of himself? Would he cry "Havock!" and let slip the dogs of war? Miss Skinner started at the unexpected sound, and turned and looked behind her.

" Those rats grow bolder every day, " she cried. " Now, where has the key of that cupboard gone? Who has dared to take the key of that cupboard? "

"I don't know, Miss Skinner, " I answered, my hand straying fearfully towards my pocket.

" Ring the bell for Mary. That key was in the lock this morning, and I'll have it found. "

I rang the bell and Mary came, but she knew nothing about the key. She searched, Miss Skinner searched, I searched, but nowhere could that key be found. It was the most extraordinary disappearance, most unaccountable, so Miss Skinner kept saying again and again. Suddenly she called out:

"Rosamund, what *have* you got bulging out in your pocket? Come here, and let me see."

I was stooping to look under a low book-shelf for the missing key at that moment, and jumped up as if I had been shot.

" Don't stand there staring at me," she called out impatiently, " come at once."

Tremblingly I came and stood before her. With ruthless hands she dived into my pocket and brought forth a large packet of sweets and the missing key!

I cannot describe the scene that followed. Miss Skinner refrained from hitting me this time, but her tongue outvenom'd all the worms of Nile. I stood before her, crimson and helpless, obstinately refusing to give any explanation as to how key and sweets came into my pocket. Mary came to the rescue at last.

" I can't think how she came by the sweets, Ma'am, " she said, " but I believe myself she locked the door because of those rats. They was making a terrible noise, and p'raps they frightened her."

" Well, why couldn't the naughty girl have said so instead of being so obstinate?" said Miss Skinner, cooling down a little at this partial explanation. "You'll sit down now, Rosamund, and do ten division sums as a punishment for your deception and obstinacy, and you'll have no supper. I shall write and tell Mrs. Hunter you can't come and play with her girls to-morrow, as we had arranged, because you are so naughty you would corrupt them. Mary, we'll poison those rats to-morrow. Remind me to do so. Come out now and leave Miss Rosamund to do her sums. Don't stir from your seat until you have done them, Rosamund."

She put the key of the cupboard and the sweets in her pocket, and went out of the room into her sanctum opposite, leaving the doors open so that she might hear if I played instead of doing my sums.

With a low "Hush" to Felix I began my task, and had soon done the sums. I never allowed Miss Skinner to find it out, because it would have meant lengthened impositions, but I was very quick at my lessons and sums. My task thus swiftly accomplished, I looked round at the cupboard, longing to be able to open it and set the prisoner free. Becoming aware that it was very silent in the enemy's sanctum I stole on tip-toe to the door and peeped in. Miss Skinner was asleep in her favourite arm-chair by the window, grunting under her weary life. I stole back to the schoolroom.

"Felix," I whispered through the key-hole, "she is asleep, so we can talk. Are you comfortable?"

"Hardly, Rosamund. I've got to play the part of a hungry rat, and it sounds very much as if I should have to remain cramped up in this dark cupboard until I'm poisoned to-morrow morning."

He spoke loud in his impatience, and the sound disturbed the grunting lady in the next room.

"Rosamund, what are you doing? Have you finished your sums?" she called out, rising and coming into the passage.

"Yes, Miss Skinner."

"Then go to bed. Walk out: I want to lock the door."

I walked out and she locked the door behind me.

"Now go to bed at once, and no pranks or playing about whilst you are undressing. If I hear any noise I shall come up to you."

O poor Felix, doubly barred and bolted now! I cried as I laid myself down to sleep in the big room with empty beds on either side of me, and my heart went out pitifully to my new-found friend, condemned for my sake to pass the night in a dark, cold, rat-haunted cupboard. Of course I could easily have released him by going to Miss Skinner and confessing all, but that I could not bring myself to do though I lay tossing uneasily and thinking of it for hours. It was easier to let Felix suffer, with shame I confess it: it was easier to let him suffer.

I dreamt that night that I went to the cupboard and found Felix dead there. So bitter was my sorrow and remorse in the dream that I broke into a sharp low cry and awoke. Even when I had awakened, the consciousness of base ingratitude, and the sense of misery were still upon me, so strong was the influence of the dream. I felt I would do anything now to save Felix, ay, even

confess to Miss Skinner. But first I must go
down and see if he were yet alive, I could do
nothing until I had heard his voice once more.
I rose, softly opened my door, and ran downstairs, bare-footed and in my thin nightdress.
The dawn was creeping in through the shutters.
Oh, how cold it was! a nipping and an eager air,
and all through the long night whilst I slept in
my warm bed, Felix, cold, hungry, and cramped,
had been standing pinned against the wall behind
the cupboard door. The schoolroom looked weird
and ghostly in the pale light. With an anxious,
wildly-beating heart I flew up to the cupboard.
It was empty. Felix had gone!

I could scarcely believe my eyes; it seemed
like the work of a magician. Amazed, I stared
around me, and then I perceived that the large
pane of glass which formed the lower part of
the window had been smashed, leaving a hole
big enough for a man to creep through. This

was no magician's work, now I saw the hand of
Felix in it all. He had waited until we were
all in bed and asleep, and then he had burst the
lock of the cupboard door, smashed the window,
and escaped. The marvel was that no one had
been awakened, but fortunately Miss Skinner's
room was at the back, where she could not have
heard the disturbance easily.

I scuttled back to bed feeling I had been
saved as well as Felix, having just sense enough
to pick up my Shakspere and lock the schoolroom
door after me.

There was much excitement in the morning
when all the bursting and smashing was discovered.
It passed, however, as an attempted burglary.
To her dying day Miss Skinner believed that the
wretch who came in through the window was
disappointed, like Mother Hubbard's dog, by find-
ing that the cupboard was bare, and receiving
a bad impression of the house at starting did not

consider it worth while to pursue his researches further. How Felix explained his late return to his grandmother I know not. It was not my wont to concern myself about what did not concern me in those days.

That afternoon, Miss Skinner, according to her usual custom, went forth to garden. She found the walks particularly verdant, notwithstanding the weeding I had given them, so I was called, railed at in good set terms, and put to work upon them.

I could not endure weeding, it hurt my hands so, but it was pleasant to be out of doors and within sight of Felix's house and garden, so I managed to get on by resting when Miss Skinner's back was turned and grabbing at the weeds with violence when she looked my way.

It was very amusing to watch Miss Skinner gardening. She became very absorbed in her work, much too absorbed to study grace of attitude. On

this occasion she was sowing some hardy annuals,
and being very short-sighted she had to bend a
good deal over the flower-beds, consequently her
skirt dragged up behind revealing a good deal
of shank.   Oh, it was very funny to watch her!
Her prominent nose nearly touched the bed, she
might have raked the ground with it, and her
thin legs scuttled about like a frightened fowl's.
Poor Miss Skinner! I indulged in a silent fit of
laughter as I watched her then, but I think of
her with a tender pity when I picture that scene
now.   Her sordid drudging life had withered
every vestige of outward grace.   Beneath its
influence she had become mean, harsh, and
unpleasing, but in her soul there must have
been some inward grace, some dormant hidden
poetry, for she loved her flowers.   They were
the only bright things in her existence, the
sole things that spoke to her of the beauty of
life.

Once I heard George Macdonald lecture on a line from Shakspere :

I see a cherub, that sees them.

To most people this is simply one of Hamlet's mad utterances, but the heavenly-minded lecturer understood better the beautiful idea. That line was a "cherub" to him through whose eyes he saw many beautiful far-off things. He became a cherub to us himself. He talked to us about Heaven. He could not make us see it, but we saw that he saw it, and as he talked, that undiscovered country, which is the goal of us all, became·very real and near. We saw it through his eyes, that was his strange power. And as he went on he developed Hamlet's idea further, and showed us that all beautiful things were cherubs through whose eyes we got glimpses of diviner things beyond. Do we not all at times feel the truth of this ? We listen to a lovely strain of music: why does it move us? What is its power? The composer himself could not tell you, he could only pass the cherub on, and we gaze through its eyes as he gazed and, if we have music in our souls, see as he saw. And that same strain becomes a cherub to countless generations. Some years ago I saw a picture that brought tears to my eyes. A peaceful sunset behind some lovely hills. I noticed that most people were silent when they stood before that picture. It was a cherub, it lifted us up, we gazed through its eyes and saw something beyond, diviner than the sunset.

Flowers were Miss Skinner's cherubs. She came and looked at them when she was weary, and they gazed back at her and gave her glimpses of a more beautiful beyond.

But these are the thoughts of later years; I must go back to myself of the early days.

CHAPTER V.

JUST as I was indulging in a fit of silent laughter over the fowl-like legs, a voice close to us called out suddenly "Good morning." We both looked up startled, and there was Felix standing quite near us, only separated from us by the low wall which divided his garden from Miss Skinner's strip of flower-beds.

"Good morning," answered Miss Skinner rather stiffly, straightening herself and making a grab at her bonnet to tilt it forward as she spoke. It was generally hanging half way down her back by the strings when she was gardening. I was so taken aback that I sat motionless amongst the weeds, and stared at Felix as if he were a madman.

"Gardening is hard work, is it not?" went on Felix pleasantly, addressing Miss Skinner, "but your garden looks so nice and well kept, I am sure it repays you for your labour."

Miss Skinner looked pleased, and regarded the young man with a more favourable eye. "I try to keep it nice and pretty," she said, "but it is hard work, as you say, with so much else to do, and I can't afford to spend much on flowers. So many things failed last year, and this year even my crocuses failed, and I love crocuses beyond every flower in the world. The soil is very bad, you come upon the chalk directly, and I've no hot-bed to raise anything in.—I do envy you your beautiful garden," she went on with a sigh, "your hyacinths and tulips are quite a show."

"I want you to accept some from me," said Felix, looking at her with bright, kind eyes.

"Please don't be offended. You see, I am a neighbour now, so we must not remain strangers. I have them here all ready."

He stooped as he spoke, reappearing a second after with a beautiful pot of tulips in each hand. These he placed upon the wall, and then dived again, bringing up this time two exquisite hyacinths.

Miss Skinner turned crimson with delight. "What beauties!" she exclaimed, "but, Sir, I really cannot rob you."

"Nonsense!" answered Felix, "you must not refuse me. We have more than we know what to do with."

Then he dived a third time, reappearing with a large basket, and said in a matter-of-fact voice: "And here are some nice flower-roots. This is a rare and very beautiful kind of dahlia, you must protect it at nights until all danger of frost is over, the gardener says. And this is the evening primrose, and these are carnations, and pinks, and here are Canterbury bells, and Michaelmas daisies, and asters, and, let me see—I think these are sunflowers. They are all fit to be planted out now, the gardener tells me, so I do hope they will succeed in your garden and give you pleasure. Next year I will see you get some crocuses, since you are so fond of them."

Miss Skinner could scarcely speak for pleasure. "Oh, but it is too much : you are too good!" she exclaimed at last, with a little gasp.

"Nonsense!" said Felix again, "a flower or two is nothing." He never could bear to be thanked. It was a peculiarity of his.

"Well, since you insist—Oh, I must, I must!" exclaimed Miss Skinner bending her flushed elderly face over the dear roots. "They will make my garden quite a blaze in the summer. I must plant them at once, at once, before they droop."

"I'll come and help you" cried Felix, leaping over the wall, and actually, though Miss Skinner had never seen him before, she made no objection.

Oh, sly Felix! The remarks he had overheard about flower-roots, when in the cupboard, had not been lost upon him. He was turning them to good account. And yet, though I knew Felix had an object in this kindness, and was deliberately trying to ingratiate himself with my guardian, I felt instinctively that he was pleased with Miss Skinner's pleasure. I sat and looked at him as he stood talking to her, and thought I had never before seen so bright and good a face. It was like the morning, and seemed to bring fresh day into my life.

" Get up, Rosamund, and speak to the young gentleman. Where are your manners? " said Miss Skinner sharply, remembering me for a moment in the midst of her excitement.

I got up and offered Felix a weedy hand. " A little orphan," I heard Miss Skinner whisper to him as I did so, and Felix said: " Oh indeed ! "

quite as if he did not know better, and had heard nothing of an absent father.

Then he and Miss Skinner began to garden, and I really think Felix became genuinely interested in the little strip of flower-beds and was honestly pleased to help their overworked owner. I began to feel interested in the garden myself, so strong is the influence of example, and handed roots with much zeal.

When they were all planted, Felix attacked the walks, and worked side by side with me whilst Miss Skinner watered her new possessions. It felt quite odd, we were so like a happy little family that afternoon. Miss Skinner became quite gentle, and weeding changed from a disagreeable task into a delightful pastime, such was the magic of Felix's genial presence.

It was a particularly bright afternoon. The cheerful spring sunshine illumined everything, the flowers in Felix's own garden flamed beneath

it, and the windows of his house shone like diamonds betwixt the trees. In front of us, beyond
the little green gate and the white road, lay the
downs, stretching away as far as the eye could
reach, with cloud shadows racing over them
towards the distant sea. Ever since that afternoon
I have loved to see cloud shadows racing over
sunlit turf. They suggest to me so many delightful things: buoyancy, freshness, coolness, swift
happy bird-like motion, youth, high spirits, and
the budding spring-time. Oh, Earth would not be
complete without her shadows! Look up, and
we see they come from Heaven: sweet soft spirits
sent from above, to emphasize the sunshine!

Of course Felix was told the whole history of
the burglary, and he was much amazed at the
audacity of the burglar, and blushed for very
shame at the thought of such a thing. He was
also very sympathetic over the broken window
and the cupboard lock.

"I tell you what, Miss Skinner," he said, "some workmen are doing odd jobs for us at the house, I'll send a couple round to-morrow to repair the window and cupboard. Please don't pay them, because they will get paid by us anyway for their day's work, and there is no reason why they should be paid twice over."

The workmen came next day, did their work, and went away again without payment—trust Miss Skinner for that. We heard no more of the burglary, and Felix was not again put to the blush.

Also, he had won Miss Skinner's heart. The sending of the workmen, in conjunction with the flower-roots, quite softened her tough fibres. I have never seen her unbend to anyone so suddenly as she did to Felix. To her pupils she was ever stiff and cold as an icicle, but I suppose we acted upon her as the east wind did upon the man in the fable, and genial warm-hearted Felix bursting upon her with gifts of flowers in his train, was like the sun.

Quite a friendship sprang up between the two, a friendship productive of much happiness to me. Scarcely a day passed that we did not see something of Felix. Whenever he saw us gardening or weeding the walks, he used to leap the wall and join us, always with a root or a flower in one hand for Miss Skinner and frequently with a little gift for me in the other. Presently he got bolder still and invaded the house with his presents, and on one occasion he was formally asked to tea, and there were hot cakes and *buttered* toast, so nice that I begged him privately to come again to tea as soon as he could. In a wonderfully short time we grew so intimate that he used to walk in without knocking, and Miss Skinner, when she was busy, actually trusted him so far as to allow him to carry me off for a morning by the sea. Oh, what happy mornings

those were, and how kind Felix was to me!
We were supposed to spend all our time on the
beach, but a good deal of it was spent at the
confectioner's, and I seldom returned hungry to
my dinner, which was most fortunate, both for
the dinner and myself.

We never saw the grandmother, Mrs. Vaughan-
Price. At first I think Miss Skinner fondly hoped
she would call, Felix being so exceedingly friendly,
but day after day passed, and she came not.
Miss Skinner at last betrayed her disappointment
to Felix, and 'twas wonderful how many polite
messages the grandmother sent after that. She
did not call, but it became understood that she
would have flown to make Miss Skinner's acquaintance had she not been subject to most distressing
headaches which invariably came on if she paid
calls. Miss Skinner was quite concerned when
she heard this and said that though she seldom
called on people first herself, being so poor,

and unable to entertain, she should break her
rule in this instance, and call on the poor invalid.
Then Felix explained, in rather an embarrassed
manner, that his grandmother's headaches came on
still more distressingly when people paid calls
upon her, so rather reluctantly Miss Skinner had
to abandon all hope of an acquaintanceship with
Mrs. Vaughan-Price.

The holidays came to an end at last, and
Felix was told by our instructress that his visits
to the house must cease.

The girls came back, and were surprised and
a little hurt to find that I had enjoyed the holidays
immensely, and was not in ecstasies over their
return. Indeed, quite a coldness sprang up between
my companions-of-the-bedchamber and myself in
consequence of my cool reception of them. They
had returned brimful of sympathy and condolence,
and prepared to " pay out old Skinner " for treating
me so unfairly, so no doubt it was disappointing

to find me cheerful. The coldness lasted for one day, and then suddenly I was rehabilitated in their favour and rose at one vast bound to the rank of heroine.

During this first day there had been no mention of Felix. I had thought of him a good deal and had lamented silently over his pleasant visits, now, alas, at an end, but I did not speak of my new-found friend to my companions, in consequence of the coldness between us. The second day was Sunday, and as usual we walked to church two and two, Miss Jones in front, and Miss Skinner behind.

I had discovered Felix's pew by this time, and contrived, when everyone's head was bowed in the Litany, to let him have a peep at a small three-cornered note in my hand. A slight nod showed me I was understood. Felix was in the porch when we came out, standing so that I had to brush by him in passing. He lifted his hat and bowed politely to Miss Skinner, and under cover of that bow I managed to slip the note into the hand that hung down by his side. 'Twas swiftly done, but girls' eyes are wondrous sharp, and my companions-of-the-bedchamber, who were nearest me, beheld the amazing deed.

No sooner had we gained our room than I was beset by a torrent of excited questions, and coldness changed to awe and admiration on the part of my companions and pleased superiority on mine.

"Be calm, girls, be calm," I said, assuming my grandest manner. "In due time all shall be revealed. You shall learn how with sweet words we lulled to sleep the insolent foe; an' if you will take an oath of secrecy, you shall be the instruments of darkness and witness deeds that will make your blood run cold."

There was no time for more as we had to go down to say the collect to the insolent foe. The afternoon was one of intense excitement. The girls could scarcely restrain their curiosity, and every act of mine was watched with interest. Perceiving this, I added fuel to the fire, by adopting much mystery of movement. I gazed out of the window and started violently at every sound without, and once I put my hand to my heart, and sank back in my chair and panted, which had a great success. Altogether 'twas a most enjoyable day, and not one hour too long for me, though I could see my companions were wildly longing for the hour of revelation.

At eight o'clock we were sent to bed by Miss Jones. Miss Skinner always went to church on Sunday evenings, so we were safely quit of her for an hour or two and we did not fear a visit from Miss Jones. She was supposed to come and see we were safely in bed; but she was engaged, and always wrote to her lover on Sunday evenings, so forgot this little duty. I felt I was mistress of the situation and when we reached our room acted accordingly.

"Silence for five minutes!" I called out arbitrarily, then sat down in an important attitude on the only chair in the room.

This was more than the girls could stand, and they became so indignant I thought it wiser not to try them any longer. Therefore I hastily made them take a solemn oath of secrecy, and plunged into my story. When I came to the part where Felix lay hidden in the cupboard whilst Miss Skinner and I took our tea a yard from the door, their excited faces were a sight to see! In fact, they refused to believe it, until I also took an oath, and swore 'twas true. Their excitement excited me and I am afraid I embellished the story a little towards the end, and smashed the window for Felix with my own hand. There was a pause of awe when I concluded, and I read in every eye that I had become a heroine and was covered with glory.

"Well, there's an adventure!" exclaimed Isabel, breaking the awed silence. "Why, you almost saved his life by going down in the dead of night to show him the way to freedom. And he too! such a swell! And living in that fine house! Is he very rich, Rosamund?"

"Rich!" I repeated scornfully. "Rich! ask the confectioner! Rich isn't the word." Then I enumerated all the different things I had eaten at Felix's expense during the holidays, and really thus summed up, they mounted into an amazingly large total.

"There's a friend to have!" said Joanna, a delicate girl who cried very often over the scanty school-fare. "I'd give something to be you, Rosamund."

"Wait a bit!" I said mysteriously, "I can call spirits from the vasty deep, and perchance they may bring something nice for you. See you this butterfly net? 'Twas given me by Felix, and now 'tis going to be a mortal engine whose rude throat shall pour forth treasures at thy feet."

I fished out a butterfly net from under my mattress as I spoke, and waved it dramatically above my head. The girls watched me spellbound, whilst I marched down the room with it and rapped deliberately with the handle on the window. There was a moment's silence and I began to feel a little anxious and to run over in my mind the contents of my note to Felix, wondering whether aught could have annoyed him or caused him to mistake place or hour. Thus my note had run:

"DEAR FELIX,

"It is miserable without you. Since *She* forbids visits to the house, jump the wall at a quarter past eight, stand under my window, and wait for a sign, then throw up gravel, and if the window opens, all is well. We can then have a long interview. And, dear Felix, if you don't mind our mentioning it, we do get so hungry. I could let down my long handled butterfly net to you, and then if you *happen* to have anything nice with you, you might tie it to the handle, but remember we are seven of us in our room, and all hungry, especially Joanna.

"Ever your loving friend,

"Rosamund."

Surely Felix would not fail me after that appeal. I could not believe it of him. And yet that moment's silence with six expectant girls gathered round me, was very trying. I rapped again. Oh, joy! Some gravel came rattling merrily against the window. I flung it open in a transport of delight.

"We are all here!" I exclaimed joyfully. "Here, girls, come and be introduced. Mr. Felix

Gray of next door, Miss Isabel Sturgeon, Joanna Buckley, May Tompkins, Lizzie, Jane, Amelia, and here's the butterfly net."

I lowered the net and the girls crowded round the window eagerly. It was a clear starlight evening, and we could see Felix distinctly, standing below, a rather dark figure amidst the little flower-beds. There was a basket on his arm. Dear kind Felix! from first to last he never failed me or refused request of mine. The basket was tied to the end of the butterfly net handle, just above the net, to prevent its slipping, and then I drew it up. Within were seven tartlets, seven slices of sponge cake, fourteen figs, unlimited biscuits, and a huge bunch of grapes. Imagine what this meant to girls like us, who never at any meal got quite enough food to satisfy our hunger. We thanked Felix most gratefully, let down the empty basket and began upon the tartlets. Felix looked up at us from where he stood amidst the flowers, and said in a soft voice that he could not bear girls to be hungry and would try to come every night at that hour with something nice for us. And when he failed to come we were to understand that he had not forgotten us, but had been obliged to return to Oxford.

Every night after that, for nearly a week, Felix came with a well-filled basket, and everything he said was so gentle and kind and pleasant, that when at last he went back to Oxford, there was not one of us who would not have died for him, in a painless way.

My position in the school was very different after this episode. In spite of the solemn oath of secrecy taken by my companions-of-the-bed-chamber, every girl in the school soon knew the whole story of Felix, and I became an object of deepest interest, and a recognized Leader.

Miss Skinner had a bad time of it this term.

Excited by my recent triumphs, I rushed into unheard-of deeds of daring, and my spirit of recklessness infected the whole school. A girl in an adjoining bedchamber to ours even went so far as to start a Felix of her own, but he was a failure, borrowed a shilling and disappeared. And well for him he never crossed his proprietress's path again, for in her mortification and anger she might have torn him joint by joint and strewn the hungry churchyard with his limbs!

I cannot give you a detailed account of the four years of school life that followed. Summer, autumn, and winter have to follow; alas! one cannot linger for ever in the spring time, the only pretty ring time. The four years would have been barren had it not been for Felix. Term after term he came back to me faithfully. He alone saved me from becoming utterly ignoble in the midst of ignoble surroundings. If ever a longing to improve inspired me, or if ever my

heart were touched into tenderness and thought
for others, 'twas Felix who touched and inspired.
Every joy and pleasure that came to me, came
through him, and every gift was brought to me
by his hand.   The history of our friendship during
these years of my early girlhood can be summed up
in four words: Felix gave, I accepted.   O Heaven!
To think of how I recompensed him afterwards!

And yet, though you may doubt it when you
read further, from the first I loved Felix.   I did
for him what I would have done for no other.
For his sake I tried to learn, and especially did
I strive to play well upon the piano.   I loved
music myself, and when Felix told me that he
sang, and hoped some day he might sing to an
accompaniment of my playing, then I spared myself
no trouble to learn, and being quick of ear and
of finger soon succeeded passing well.   Also as
I grew older I began to take more pains with
my appearance and manners.   Felix was very

point device in his accoutrements and very gentle in his speech, and it seemed to pain him when I appeared before him with tangled locks and grubby hands, flinging myself about, and saying every rude and careless thing that came into my head. When I think of what I was in those days, I wonder often what Felix could have seen in me that he should have remained so long my willing slave, but I suppose I had a fascination for him as I have had since for many others. And then I was singularly pretty. He told me so on one occasion. It was Sunday evening and holiday time, and we were together in Miss Skinner's little strip of garden. He told me that I was like a fair, beautiful flower that spoiled herself wilfully, and he wished I would hold my head up to heaven and not lay me down in the dust.

" I don't lie down in the dust," I said poutingly. " I can't help it if my frock is dusty and shabby Miss Skinner wrote to uncle and told him my wardrobe needed renovating, but he took no notice of her letter, so I have to go on wearing old clothes."

"You don't quite understand what I mean, Rosamund," he said gently. "Never mind your shabby frock, you can't help that, the most beautiful flowers have rough sheaths. But look at this hair,"—he took up a tangled mass as he spoke— "if you brushed this out it would be like threads of gold; the sunshine can't get into it now, it is so matted. And look at your hands, small pretty delicate hands, but I seldom see them clean."

"We are not allowed to waste the soap," I replied, snatching my hands from him and executing a *pas seul* on the gravelled walk. I always took to dancing when Felix lectured me, because it annoyed him, and made him leave off.

"I am sure that is not true, Rosamund," said Felix, "I have heard Miss Skinner send you upstairs to wash them many a time."

"I thank you for your voices, thank you, your most sweet voices," I answered, mocking him as proud Coriolanus mocked the citizens, and then I changed the dance to a particularly inelegant one of my own invention: a waddle up the middle path, ladies' chain round the handle of the pump at the end of the garden, down the middle on one leg, and *chassez* to right and left with back turned to partner. Felix watched me gravely, then without a word, took off his hat and left me.

That was ever his way when I was naughty. He left me to heaven, and to those thorns that in our bosoms lodge, to prick and sting us. And though I could not bear him to leave me, I drove him to it many a time, ay, once too often. The thorns pricked and stung me on this occasion. I had mocked, but I had been ashamed for all that.

Next time Felix saw me, my hair was flowing far below my waist, in loose untangled glory, and I felt

with delight as I stood in the bright spring sunshine that it was like threads of gold, and that
my palms and finger-tips were rosy from the
kisses of fresh cold water. I saw Felix's eyes
light up with pleasure and admiration as he
looked at me, and personal vanity awoke within
my breast. I began to take pains with myself
in order to make Felix admire me. My rough
sheath I could not help, but I took care the flower
should be as spotless and beautiful as care could
make it. Also I tried to move and speak more
gently, but this I found very difficult, for my
spirits ran away with me continually, and, indeed,
to this day I relapse occasionally into the old
wildness.

Yes, certainly I did for Felix what I would
have done for no other. I cried bitterly every
time he went back to Oxford, and I felt mad
with joy when he returned again. We were
more and more together as we grew older, for

Miss Skinner allowed me more freedom, or perhaps I took it, and she became so fond of Felix
that she could refuse him nothing. So he came
to the house when he listed, and took me out
for walks when he chose, and we met besides
many a time she knew not of.

The last year of my school life was decidedly
the happiest. Felix left Oxford, having taken
honours, and spent a long holiday at home, so
I saw him daily. I told him one day how dearly
I loved reciting, and he insisted on giving me
lessons in the art. Miss Skinner made no objection, so a lady was found to teach me. She came
twice a week and a surprisingly good instructress
she proved. I got on so wonderfully that soon
rumours of my performances spread abroad, and
Miss Skinner received frequent letters from
clergymen and others, begging that I might be
allowed to recite for them at little entertainments
got up for charitable purposes. These requests

were refused, partly because my clothes were so
poor and shabby, and partly because Miss Skinner feared my uncle might disapprove if it came
to his ears that I had performed in public. But
at length, quite at the end of my last term, the
very day on which most of the girls went home,
came an invitation which was not refused.

CHAPTER VI.

THIS most surprising invitation was actually from the headachy Mrs. Vaughan-Price. Words cannot describe the commotion in Miss Skinner's breast when the note arrived. It ran as follows:

"DEAR MISS SKINNER,

" A few friends are coming to spend the afternoon with me to-morrow at four o'clock, and have a great desire to hear your pupil recite. I believe my grandson has the pleasure of your acquaintance; I therefore venture to ask you to join our party and bring the little girl with you. Kindly reply this evening.

Yours truly,

ANASTASIA VAUGHAN-PRICE.

"To-morrow, that is the 14th of April, how fortunate your uncle does not want you until the 15th, we shall be able to go now!" exclaimed Miss Skinner, her hands so tremulous with excitement that the note she held wagged up and down like a leaf in a gale.

"I shan't go," I said. "The proud old thing only asks me because she wants me to amuse her friends. She has taken no notice of me all these four years. 'Little girl' indeed! I am not a little girl, and I have no intention of being treated like one."

But Miss Skinner did not see that the invitation was not a flattering one, or if she did, put her pride in her pocket and seemed determined to go. She said if I recited there it would be a very good advertisement for her school, and it would not be like performing in public, so my uncle could not object. I objected to being an advertisement, and then she said I was very selfish, and wondered how I could refuse an opportunity of seeing so beautiful a house and garden. Seeing her heart was so set on going, I yielded so far as to say that I, too, should like to see the house Felix lived in, but that I would not go there in shabby clothes. And here the matter rested, for much as Miss Skinner longed to go, her desire was not strong enough to prompt her to furbish me up at her own expense.

In the afternoon Felix came in and asked rather anxiously if we were going to accept his grandmother's invitation.

"You'd better ask Rosamund," answered Miss Skinner sharply, "I can do nothing with her, she's so vain and obstinate."

"I am not vain and obstinate," I said indignantly, "but I won't let my candied tongue lick absurd pomp, and I am not going to see Felix's grandmother in a bulged sailor hat, and shoes burst at the toes."

Then Felix said he was most anxious for many reasons that I should accept his grandmother's invitation, and make a good impression upon her, and he said if I would only come out with him to choose the things he would give me a new hat and shoes and anything else necessary. By this time I had become so used to Felix's gifts that I had no shame in accepting anything from him, so I put on my bulged hat and burst shoes and sallied forth by his side. Miss Skinner let us depart without a word. She was glad the matter had been thus pleasantly settled without any call upon her own pocket.

First we sought for and found a hat shop. I was much taken with a grey velvet bonnet trimmed with feathers, and long ribbons to tie under the chin. It struck me as the kind of head-gear likely to make a good impression upon the grandmother. But the shopwoman smiled when I tried it on, and Felix agreed with her that

'twas too matronly looking for a young girl. A
large gauzy looking black hat was next tried on.

"Ah! The young lady really looks lovely in
this!" exclaimed the shopwoman, "it makes her
face look so fair, and sets off the golden hair."

Without more ado, the hat was bought, and
an expensive one it proved, costing Felix two
and a half guineas. Then we went to a shoe-
maker's, and bought a sweet little pair of buckled
shoes; and Felix having espied a hole in my
stocking whilst I was trying the shoes on, we
next repaired to a draper's, where I bought a
pair of black silk stockings, a pair of light kid
gloves, and an embroidered pocket-handkerchief.
We then agreed that my dress was much too
shabby to wear with such smart appointments,
and at Felix's request, some ready-made dresses
were shown us. They were none of them quite
the right thing; but at last we hit upon a very
pretty pale green silk skirt, and the girl who

served us, having become quite interested in our purchases, promised to make me a bodice to it by the following morning. She took my measurements, and we happily turned homewards when all was done.

"Most complete I shall be now," I said gaily, as we walked down the pavement. "I ought to make a good impression on your grandmother; don't you think so?"

"I hope so," answered Felix earnestly. "A great deal depends upon it, Rosamund dear. I scarcely like to tell you how much depends upon it, you still seem so much a child."

This speech annoyed me. In many ways, no doubt, I was still very much a child, for I knew nothing whatsoever of the world beyond Miss Skinner's school, and I still wore my hair flowing over my shoulders, and my frocks, which I had outgrown, were very short, which made me seem younger than my years. Nevertheless, I was verging on seventeen and taller than any girl in the school, so it was mortifying in one day to be called both a little girl and a child.

"I am very, very anxious my grandmother should think well of you," went on Felix, " so even if you find her a little stiff and difficult to get on with, try, dear, to be sweet and pleasant to her, for my sake. You'll do this for Felix, will you not?"

"Of course I will," I answered shortly, "why should you be afraid, you solemn old thing." Then catching sight of his anxious face, my heart softened and I added—"I'm provoking sometimes, but I always do what you wish me to do in the end, don't I, Felix?"

"In the end," he repeated, half laughingly, " that may not always do, Rosamund. There is no time like the golden Now. But we will not be solemn any longer, or I shall end by making you quite nervous about to-morrow. Come, here's the confectioner's. We can't pass without turning in, such conduct would be without a precedent."

We turned in to the confectioner's and had a feast, a farewell feast, for in two days I should be leaving the familiar haunts of my girlhood. Some girls might have felt sad, but as we walked home I almost skipped along the pavement by Felix's side, 1 felt so happy. It was such a lovely afternoon, and I was so pleased to think that the next day I should be going to a real party, dressed in pretty things, and Felix looked so kind and indulgent and so pleased with my pleasure. Oh, how long ago it seems! It was the spring time then, the spring time, the only pretty ring time. Dark days, December bareness were very far away.

At four o'clock the next afternoon Miss Skinner and I assembled in the schoolroom, dressed for the party. Miss Skinner wore her best black silk and jet-trimmed mantle and had a new feather, purple this time, in her bonnet, and wide lace ruffles hanging over her wrists instead of the red mittens. I was robed from head to foot in the gifts of Felix. The green silk skirt proved to be a little short for me, but the bodice fitted beautifully. Miss Skinner looked at me again and again, as though slightly surprised at the appearance I presented.

"You look very nice, Rosamund," she said as we started, "very nice indeed. But for goodness' sake don't put your hand in your pocket and swing your skirt about as you walk. It's short enough when it's left alone, but when you swing it about it's disgraceful."

I continued to swing it about as I walked, calmly superior in the consciousness of silk stockings and pretty buckled shoes.

"I must beg you'll behave yourself when you get to the party," went on Miss Skinner, getting exasperated. "You'll shock Mrs. Vaughan-Price if you put on your hoity-toity airs. Remember now, you're to keep quiet, and mind you get up to recite directly you're asked, and above all don't cross your legs, as you're so fond of doing. I shall scrape my throat like this—H—h—hem—if I see you doing anything wrong, then you'll know what I mean."

I began to feel impatient. It seemed to me that both Felix and Miss Skinner were making an unnecessary fuss over my behaviour at the party. .

"Mrs. Vaughan-Price has asked *me*," I said poutingly, "why should I behave like somebody else? I shall not use an enforcèd ceremony, or hang a calf's skin on these recreant limbs."

"There you are! Why can't you talk in your own language instead of dragging in that old Shakspere every minute? Upon my word, strangers must think you are demented."

We had reached Felix's door by this time, to my great relief, for Miss Skinner's prattle was becoming a little tedious. She rang the bell, and a butler flung it open, I thought in rather a proud manner. We could see a large hall behind him, and two footmen in gay livery waiting at the bottom of the stairs. Miss Skinner suddenly became nervous and lost her presence of mind.

"Is Mrs. Praughan-Vice at home?" she asked in a shaky voice.

"*Mrs. Vaughan-Price* is at home," answered the butler with great distinctness. Miss Skinner walked in with all the dignity she could muster, and then the butler caught sight of me.

"Miss Gwynne?" he said inquiringly, with a sudden look of interest.

"Miss Skinner and Miss Gwynne," put in my instructress pointedly.

The butler moved aside to a table and returned with a lovely large posy of daffodils. "With Mr. Felix's compliments," he said, putting it into my hands. There was a little card lying

amidst the golden heads of the flowers. I took
it up and read: "For Rosamund to hold in her
hands whilst she is reciting." I felt quite giddy
with pleasure. No prima donna in the flush of
her greatest triumph ever felt prouder that I as
I followed the gay footmen and Miss Skinner
upstairs, behind my bunch of glowing nodding
daffodils. Miss Skinner turned to me looking
very red, when she reached the top of the stairs.
" Mind you behave. Is my bonnet straight? "
she whispered nervously.

" Oh, yes! Do go on, Miss Skinner," I answered,
excited and impatient, " see, they are waiting and
holding the door open."

Miss Skinner entered the drawing-room, nearly
tripping over the door-mat in her agitation. The
great moment had arrived, we were at the party,
our names had been called out loudly so that
everyone might know, another second, and we
were in the middle of the party, and Felix was

threading his way to us through a crowd of people. It was a beautiful room, full of palms, statues, lovely pictures, old china, and delicate, softly hanging draperies, and the atmosphere was almost heavy with the scent of flowers.

"I am so glad you have come," said Felix, looking at me with an exceedingly pleased and proud expression, "let me take you to my grandmother."

He led us up to a sofa, on which a very stately looking old lady was sitting, surrounded by quite a court, and showing no trace of headache. Miss Skinner was introduced, received a frigid shake of the hand, and was given a chair a little distance away from the lady of the house. And there the poor thing sat, looking red and uncomfortable, most of the afternoon, and from first to last small notice was taken of her by anyone save Felix. I was introduced next, and I saw a look of surprise on the haughty face of the old lady as she shook hands with me, a look that was immediately followed by a frown. I stood before her, feeling a little shy, for she said nothing kind to set me at my ease, and I saw she was taking stock of every detail of my appearance from my hat to my buckled shoes. A gentleman sitting near her came to the rescue at last, with a kind remark.

"What beautiful daffodils you have," he said, "I am so fond of daffodils."

I forgot my shyness instantly. "So am I," I answered, turning to him eagerly, "they are my favourite flowers. They come before the swallow dares, and take the winds of March with beauty."

There was a look of surprise on all the faces surrounding me when I finished my quotation, and Miss Skinner scraped her throat meaningly.

"She is not a child: what did you mean by saying she was a child?" said the old lady in a loud undertone to Felix, who was standing near her.

"She is still almost a child," said Felix, getting very red.

"Old enough to be dangerous," said the gentleman who had first addressed me, speaking in a loud undertone like the old lady. She frowned again. Her frowns made me uncomfortable. Instinctively I moved towards Felix, feeling sure there would be no frowns from that quarter.

"It was so kind of you to get these daffodils for me, Felix," I said, suddenly remembering he had not been thanked. "Fancy, almost everything I have on has been given to me by you."

"Hush!" whispered Felix warningly.

The warning came too late. I had spoken in a clear voice, and I saw by Mrs. Vaughan-Price's angry, astonished face that she had heard.

She stared at both of us until Felix became crimson, and then she said: "Felix, I see Angharad looking very dull in that corner, will you oblige me by going to talk to her."

Felix reluctantly moved away from my side. "I'll come too," I said eagerly.

"Miss Gwynne, will you please take this chair," said Mrs. Vaughan-Price in an icy voice, pointing to a chair near her sofa.

I was beginning to feel very angry with the old lady, her manner was so indescribably rude, but my courage had not yet mounted to the occasion, so I seated myself on the chair pointed out to me, between a smart young lady, and a sleepy looking old gentleman.

"You've come to recite, have you not?" asked the young lady, eyeing me very superciliously.

I did not like her question, or her manner, so I looked back at her as superciliously and said: "Yes, paid by the hour. What have you come to do?"

For answer she turned her back upon me. Then for a long time I sat silent. The old gentleman took no notice of me whatever, no one took any notice of me except the gentleman who had said I was old enough to be dangerous, and he confined himself to staring. Mrs. Vaughan-Price took care Felix should not approach me. Twice he drew near, and each time she sent him away on some pretext or other, before he could address a word to me. It was a most disappointing party, a horrible party, I wished a thousand times over I had never come. I looked at Miss Skinner, sitting opposite me, silent and neglected, and knew by her flushed face and mortified expression that she was thinking the same thing. A wild longing to revenge myself on the old lady for her rude reception of us, surged up in my breast, and I boiled with rage behind my daffodils. At length, tired of silence, I turned and addressed the sleepy old gentleman.

"It's very nice out to-day" I observed.

"Eh! What?" he said, turning slowly towards me, "speak louder, Missy, I'm a little deaf."

"It's very nice out to-day," I repeated.

"Oh, indeed! You saw a nice trout to-day. Whereabouts did you see it?"

"I said—'It's nice out to-day,'" I repeated, still louder.

"Yes, I heard: you saw a nice trout to-day. I asked—Whereabouts did you see it?"

The conversation seemed scarcely worth keeping up, so leaning weariedly back in my chair, I merely answered by a mumble.

"Eh! what? Speak a little louder, Missy."

The comic side of the situation began to strike me. I tried to mumble again, but the mumble turned irresistibly into a giggle. People began to look my way with rather astonished expressions, Mrs. Vaughan-Price turned a freezing look upon me, Miss Skinner scraped her throat loudly and the old gentleman drew back, evidently offended. I knew I was behaving badly, and a second scrape from Miss Skinner made me conscious that I was sitting with my legs crossed, but I had got into one of my reckless moods now, and all desire to behave well had left me. A wave of silence passed through the room, a silence that seemed awkward at a party. Mrs. Vaughan-Price broke it by addressing me, very stiffly :

"Miss Gwynne, we have heard a good deal of your powers of recitation," she said, "will you oblige us with something ?"

Miss Skinner looked anxious and gave a very loud H—h—hem. A capital idea occurred to me. That horrid old grandmother should bite the dust ; her detestable party should be made a jest for ever.

"Certainly," I answered meekly; "shall I begin now ?"

"Wait a moment," said Mrs. Vaughan-Price, relaxing a little the severity of her expression, "we must have silence before you can begin."

Silence was then commanded, and the guests collected and made a ring round me. Felix was amongst them, but I was too busy with thoughts of revenge to heed him now. I heard Mrs. Vaughan-Price say in her loud undertone—"She is very good, and very difficult to secure, quite an extraordinary talent," and then everyone looked expectantly at me. I rose, tucked my daffodils under my arm, stuck my hand into my pocket, and swinging my skirt to and fro, began in the dull monotonous sing-song of a Sunday-school child:

"Gin! Gin! a drop of Gin!
When, darkly, adversity's days set in,
And the ragged pauper, cold within,
Steep'd in poverty up to the chin,
Hardly acknowledg'd by kith and kin,
      Alas, poor rat,
      Has no cravat,
A seedy coat, and a hole in that,
No sole to his shoe, and no brim to his hat,
Not a change of linen, except his skin,
      No credit, no cash,
      No mutton to hash,
No bread, not even potatoes to mash,
   Gin! Gin! A drop of Gin!
'Tis then your *tremendous* temptations begin!"

There was a moment's dead silence when I finished, broken by giggles from some of the younger members of the party, and fearful scrapings from Miss Skinner. I looked at the old grandmother. Angry discomfiture was written on every line of her face. The whirligig of Time had speedily brought in his revenges, and her party had been made a jest for ever.

"Rosamund!" cried Miss Skinner, fussing up to me with a very red face, how could you choose such a piece!—For goodness' sake."—she whispered —"don't be so wild and naughty; even Shakspere would have been better than that." Then she continued aloud—"Do recite that pretty little piece 'The Magic Wand.'"

I looked down, slightly ashamed of myself, but not inclined to yield.

"Rosamund!" said Felix's voice. I looked up and met his eyes fixed upon me anxiously and entreatingly. Some compunctious visitings of nature almost shook my fell purpose when I saw those entreating eyes, but I did not yield. I resumed my seat, and so refused the first favour Felix had ever asked of me.

Seeing there was nothing further to be expected of me, the company dispersed about the room again. Mrs. Vaughan-Price gave me a withering look, then turned her back upon me, the kindest thing she had done yet.

" I think we'd better go home," said Miss Skinner, looking almost ill with chagrin.

"Oh, you must not take Miss Gwynne away until she has had some tea," said the gentleman who had spoken to me when I first entered the room.

I looked at Felix. He turned to Miss Skinner and took no notice of me.

" Do come and have some tea, Miss Skinner," he said, offering his arm to her as if she had been a princess. " You must not dream of going yet, we shall be having some music presently."

They walked away together, and I was left to the care of the stranger. He took a chair by my side when they had gone, and asked me a great many questions about myself, seeming especially interested in the history of my acquaintanceship with Felix.

"I think it is a fortunate thing for Felix that you are leaving Exbourne so soon," he remarked presently.

"Why?" I asked, surprised.

"Well, you see, the old lady has her plans for her grandson, and it would go ill with Felix if you thwarted them."

"But what have I to do with her plans?" I asked wonderingly.

He looked at me with a laugh. "Did Felix give you those daffodils?" he asked, without answering my question.

"Yes," I answered. "Do you like my hat?

He gave me that too—Why do you laugh so?" I added, seeing him with difficulty suppressing his laughter.

"Come to tea," he said, jumping up, "we are attracting grandmamma's attention."

We went into an adjoining room where the most delicious things were spread upon a large table, and found Felix there, still waiting upon Miss Skinner.

"Felix looks dull and out of spirits," observed my cavalier.

I had already seen that for myself, but I did not allow it to affect my spirits, and began to jest with my companion as if I were enjoying myself immensely.

"Rosamund!" whispered Miss Skinner, coming up to me nervously, "do be careful. That's the son of a Lord you're talking to."

Far from checking my merriment this news only increased it. I turned and asked my companion if his father were Lord Tomnoddy, and he said yes, and his grandfather was Duke Humphrey, and we laughed so noisily over this that soon everyone in the room was looking at us. Felix glanced at me, a glance in which pained disapproval could be read plainly, then again offered his arm to Miss Skinner and led her back to the drawing-room. Someone began playing a nocturne of Chopin's. I suddenly felt tired of my companion, who had begun paying me outrageous compliments.

"Let us go and listen to the music," I said.

"First give me your Wildacre address," said he.

I gave it him, and when he had written it down in his note-book he told me his name was D'Arcy Leigh, and hoped I would not forget him. Then he led me to the drawing-room, and we seated ourselves on a couple of chairs near the piano. But Felix kept aloof from me, and never once looked my way.

The music was very inferior. I knew I could

have done much better, and felt rather inclined to perform, but no one asked me to do so, which, considering the circumstances, was not surprising. First a very buxom looking-lady, not young, rose and went to the piano, and D'Arcy Leigh whispered to me that she was a widow, whose husband had been kindly removed to a happier sphere. With much spirit she sang a song beginning "Awake, I am free! I am free!" and I caught D'Arcy Leigh deliberately winking at the gentleman who was turning over the leaves for her. Then an elderly gentleman played the first movement of the Moonlight Sonata, very pizzi-cato in the treble, and with thumps in the bass that made you start, and after that he played something jiggy which he said was Haydn, but which would certainly have provoked a posthumous "Surprise" from that musician had it been played near his burial place. Then Mrs. Vaughan-Price said suddenly :

"Felix, it is your turn now, sing something for us."

Through the room ran a stir, and cries of "Oh do!" Felix went to the piano, and began turning over some music. I left my seat, and came softly to his side, crimson with excitement. I had never heard Felix sing, but I felt instinctively he would sing well, and I was sure he would ask me to play his accompaniment. For years I had worked hard at the piano, with the hope of such a moment as this before me, and my whole frame thrilled with delight at the thought that now --at last— the moment had come. I saw Felix look round as if in search of someone, and thinking he did not see me I whispered eagerly :

"I am here, Felix, ready to play it."

"No, thank you, Rosamund," answered Felix coldly. "I must have someone I can depend upon. Angharad, will you kindly play the accompaniment of this song of Sullivan's for me?"

A girl he had talked to a great deal, a stately dark-eyed girl, advanced to the piano. I fell back, cut to the heart, and leaned against the wall with my head hung down low over my daffodils to hide the hot tears that sprang to my eyes. It was the bitterest blow my young life had yet experienced, and I was amazed that Felix should have dealt it.

CHAPTER VII.

UPON my pain and amazement broke Felix's voice on a high, beautiful note that rang through the room, then dropped into a strain that had a dying fall. I thrilled all over as the song began, for the words were Shakspere's, I knew them well:

> Orpheus with his lute made trees
> And the mountain tops that freeze,
>   Bow themselves when he did sing.
> To his music plants and flowers,
> Ever sprung: as sun and showers
>   There had made a lasting spring.

Everything that heard him play,
Even the billows of the sea,
　Hung their heads, and then lay by.
In sweet music is such art,
Killing care and grief of heart
　Fall asleep, or hearing, die.

Again that high, beautiful note, followed by
the strain that had a dying fall. I lost all consciousness of the room in which I was standing.
I seemed to be amongst the mountains, and Felix's
voice was the voice of Orpheus, calling to me,
calling to all nature. Then came a smooth soft
strain, and the voice was like a voice in a dream,
and from over the mountains I seemed to feel
the soft south wind murmuring gently in my ear.
Louder and louder swelled voice and music, all
nature was awakening and answering: at last I
could hear even the billows of the sea replying.
Onward they rolled, ever more and more majestic,
whilst the divine voice rose and fell and rose
again, now lost in the tumult, now triumphing

over it.   At last came one supreme note, like the
call of a trumpet, and then suddenly the sea was
silent.   The voice was no longer calling, it was
dying away, receding further and further amongst
the mountains.   The answering music grew fainter
and fainter ; nature had fallen asleep, or, hearing
that sweet music, had died.   Further, still further,
receded the voice, then suddenly like the sea it
was silent, and I awoke to find that the Orpheus
who had called to me was—Felix.

Never shall I forget him as he appeared to
me at that moment.   He might have been the
son of Apollo as he stood there facing us all,
with his head thrown back, one foot planted
proudly forward, and the inspiration of song light-
ing up his face.   Let me try to describe him as
he appeared then.   His hair was bright chestnut
and curly, his eyes were brown with golden lights,
and shone beneath his straight dark brows, his
complexion was fresh and bright, his mouth firm.

and sweet, and there was both strength and grace in his tall figure. But all this can give you no idea of Felix: I cannot describe his face, never have I seen another possessing such a charm. Perhaps his most striking characteristic was his marvellous look of brightness and youth. Oh, to think that that look should ever have faded! Bright youth should be immortal; pray God it may be so in the next world, and that there we may find a lasting spring.

There was a moment of thrilled silence when the song ended, then the people burst into a storm of thanks and applause.

"I am delighted to think I have been able to give you all so much pleasure," said Felix simply, when the applause was over, and then his eyes met mine, and suddenly his face changed. I don't know what he read in my expression, but my heart felt bursting. Sudden shame came rushing upon me like the wind. Felix's simple

words which revealed his character, revealed also
my own. His chief joy was to give pleasure.
He had said it, and oh! did I not know it? For
years he had come to me with pleasures in his
hand, a faithful, never-failing friend, and not once
until to-day had he asked me to do a thing for
him. And what had I done to-day when the
golden opportunity came? Insulted his grandmother, insulted his guests, insulted him! A
great sob rose in my throat, and I rushed from
the room like a wild thing. The astonished footmen moved aside that I might descend the stairs,
but I could not face them. I turned aside and fled
along the corridor, down a steep narrow staircase,
and out through an open doorway into the fresh air.

For a moment I could see nothing, then through
my tears I saw I was in Felix's beautiful garden.
The spring sunshine was all around me, sweet
scents filled the air, brilliant flowers bloomed in
all directions, but my blurred eyes saw every-

thing through a mist, and pain filled my soul
The song had stirred me to depths I knew not
in myself. It seemed to me that for years Felix
had been calling to me in the language of a
beautiful song, and I had made no answer.
Would he be silent now? Would he cease to
try to draw me to him?

No, not yet. Felix himself was my answer.
A kind hand clasped mine suddenly, the same
kind hand that had clasped mine four long years
ago when I was a hungry child weeping for
loneliness on the sea shore. I seized it in both
my own, and placed it upon my breast, and then,
scarcely knowing what I said or did, I poured
forth my heart to my dearest friend.

"Oh, Felix!" I cried, "you do not know my
grief of heart. You have called to me so many
years and I have made no answer. And even
to-day when I came into your home, covered
with your gifts, I would not answer when you

entreated me, I would not do even one little thing for you. Oh, Felix! I began to think you would never call to me again. Your song pierced my heart, the song that *she* played for you! Forgive me, Felix, I will never behave so again; I will answer when you call, I will come to you, and follow you, and do anything in the world for you"—

Felix would not let me say more. He put my hand inside his arm, and drew me on amidst the flowers.

"Don't cry, dearest one, don't cry," he kept saying. But my tears still fell until at last, looking up, I saw Felix was looking radiantly happy, and then I began to feel happier myself. Still further he drew me amidst the flowers, and then he stooped and kissed me, not once, but many times.

"You love me a little then, Rosamund?" he asked, with a tremble in his voice.

"Better than the whole world. I found it out

when you were singing. I feel now I would follow you into another world if you called me."

Felix gave a happy laugh. "Now indeed do I feel like Orpheus," he said, "for with my lute have I won Eurydice."

"Yes," I said, "you drew me, as Orpheus drew the savage beasts of the forest. You drew all the wildness out of me. But I don't think it was the song alone, Felix. You are music yourself, you are sweet singing, you are bright spring sunshine. Your lute is your own kind nature; 'twas that, as well as the song, that touched me."

"Oh, hush! You must not be so extravagant, Rosamund. If you put me on such an extravagantly high pedestal, I shall topple over at your feet. There, smile again! I do not like to see my Rosamund weeping. Come and look at the flowers."

So saying, he drew me on into Fairyland. Nowhere have I seen a garden like this of

Felix's. It contained everything that was beautiful. Even the soft music of water was not wanting, for a brook ran murmuring by. Care and order prevailed, yet nothing was stiff or formal. Stretches of grass mingled with gay flower-beds, flowering shrubs bordered the pathways, here and there a beautiful group of trees stood proudly on the sward, and rustled their green leaves against the breezy sky. Flowers bloomed in every direction. Purple and white hyacinths, gold and crimson tulips, bright ranunculuses, softly tinted anemones, velvety auriculas, all the beautiful favourites of the spring, were there. And the wild flowers of the field and forest were there too; they had not been forgotten in Felix's garden. Golden daffodils waved and nodded on the green turf beneath the rustling trees, all along the sides of the brook grew pale sweet primroses and forget-me-nots, and lurking in corners were daisies pied, and cowslips, and delicate wood

anemones, and violets, dim, but sweeter than the
lids of Juno's eyes or Cytherea's breath.   Far off,
beyond the bordering wall, could be seen the
downs, undulating in the sunshine, and flecked
by purple shadows; whilst overhead the white
clouds raced across the blue sky, driven swiftly
onwards by the fresh sweet breath of spring.

"Oh, Felix, this is beautiful," I cried delightedly,
"you have been here with your lute."

Felix smiled, and we seated ourselves on a
grassy knoll beneath a flowering lilac tree, and
listened to the murmuring brook, and to the
thrushes and blackbirds singing for joy that spring
had come.   I felt more than ever that I loved
Felix.

"Everything that heard your music has blos-
somed," I went on, still clinging to the idea that
had filled my mind.   "Felix, here you have made
a lasting spring."

"No, not lasting," said Felix almost sadly,

"no spring is lasting. My springtime is passing away, leaving me, like you, Rosamund."

"But, Felix, when I go to-morrow I don't say good-bye to you for ever!" I exclaimed, aghast at the mere thought.

Felix laughed at the monstrous idea. "Do you think I could live without you now, Rosamund?" he said fondly. "No, I shall say good-bye to you at the station to-morrow, but it will be only good-bye for a while. My Oxford days are over now, and soon I shall be much in London reading for the Bar, so it will be easy to run down to Wildacre."

"And what will your grandmother say if she finds out you do that?"

Felix looked grave. "You have made my position a difficult one," he said slowly.

This was the only reproach he ever gave me.

"I am so sorry, Felix dear," I said, creeping up close to him. But I did not in the least realize the full significance of his words. Later, that speech of his returned to my mind, and I knew what that fatal afternoon cost Felix.

We sat a long time in that paradise of a garden, but at last Felix said it was absolutely necessary he should go back to his guests. We parted by the low wall, close to Miss Skinner's flower-beds, and I again baptized the flowers at my feet with my tears. But they were not bitter tears, for our real parting was to be on the morrow, and after all, 'twas the spring time, the only pretty ring time, and summer was coming, I hoped with many merry meetings.

Felix put me over the garden wall, and I ran back to the shabby house which had been my home for so many years. Miss Skinner was sitting in the easy chair which always stood in the window of her sanctum, a window that commanded a view of her flower-beds. She sat there a good deal, gazing out of the window, and I used to

wonder what she thought of, she always, at such
times, looked so melancholy.

" Well!" she exclaimed, when I presented myself,
"I hope you are properly ashamed of yourself.
I know I am ashamed of you. *You'll* never get
asked inside those doors again. A nice return
to make Felix for all his kindness, and he so
anxious you should make a good impression,
and giving you all those pretty things on purpose
that you might show well before his grandmother
and his friends. You put him to regular shame.
I never in my life saw Felix so down as when
he took me into the tea room."

It is strange what different effects different
people produce upon us. I had thrilled and wept
beneath Felix's voice and eyes, I waxed angry
beneath the blows of Miss Skinner's tongue.

Instead of making any excuses or apologies, I
turned my back upon her and stared into the empty
fire-place. Miss Skinner became still more incensed.

"Can't you speak?" she cried angrily. "Well,
I'll tell you what I think of you. Either you're
a fool, or you're the biggest child I ever saw.
Couldn't you see how important this afternoon
was to you? Why, if you had taken Mrs. Vaughan-
Price's fancy, there's no knowing what might
have happened, with Felix so fond of you. As
it is, the best thing he can do is to wash his hands
of you, it's thankless work to be your slave. "

I gave a half angry laugh, feeling very sure
of my slave, yet a little uneasy about the future.

"I expect he compared you very unfavourably
with his cousin, the heiress," went on Miss Skinner with marked emphasis, "she was a pretty,
nice, ladylike girl, and she played that accompaniment beautifully."

"Was that girl Angharad his cousin,—the
heiress to Cwmcoch Hall?" I asked, facing my
governess abruptly, with my cheeks aflame.

"Yes, the girl his grandmother intends him to

marry," replied Miss Skinner, looking at me with a curious intent expression.

"She wasn't a bit pretty," I cried vehemently, "and I hate nice ladylike girls, and so does Felix, I am sure. I could have played that accompaniment much better than she did. And I hate that old grandmother, and don't want her to take a fancy to me. Her headaches were all bosh, and she could have called on us years ago if she had not been a proud stuck-up old thing."

Then I burst into tears and rushed out of the room, upstairs to my bedroom. I remember now that Miss Skinner was very kind to me when I came down again, kinder and more gentle than I had ever known her, but it did not strike me much at the time, my mind was so full of other things.

Next morning I was all eagerness and excitement, packing for Wildacre. No black bag was possible this time; I had to take all my belongings with me to my new home. Miss Skinner came and helped me to pack, and was so strangely silent I looked at her in astonishment several times, wondering what had gone wrong. A little before the hour of starting came a note from Felix saying he could not come and say good-bye to me at the station, because his grandmother had particularly requested he would accompany her and her friends to Berry Point, and they were starting immediately. This was disappoint-. ing; but the letter was so loving, and held out such bright hopes of a speedy meeting, that it brought its own consolation with it. Half an hour later I was ready for my journey.

"Come into the schoolroom and have some refreshment," said Miss Skinner, when all was done.

I followed her in, and on the middle table was a nice little dish of sandwiches, and, oh, unheard-of luxury! a glass of sherry. I sat down on

the time-honoured bench, feeling that Miss Skinner was sending me off in style, and no mistake,
and began to eat, laughing and talking the while
in the highest spirits. The very thought of the
railway journey was a pleasurable excitement to
me, who for five long years had never been out
of Exbourne. Miss Skinner was seated at the
head of the narrow table, still very silent.

Suddenly she said in a trembling voice: "You've
been five years in this house, Rosamund, for five
years it has been your home——and yet, you're
glad to go."

I looked up from my sandwiches, startled and
embarrassed.

"Well, you see, Miss Skinner, it's been school,"
I said apologetically, "and now it's going to be
holidays."

"Oh, yes! That's what all you young people
think! You think life is going to be one long
holiday. It won't be. I thought as you do once,

but it's been no holiday to me. It's been drudging, thankless, toilsome work. It's been a mean life without any beauty in it. It's taken all the strength and spirit out of me, and made me a hard, unlovely old woman before my time. An old woman that no one is sorry to leave. Oh! it's not only you, Rosamund, you've all been the same; term after term you've gone away and not one kind thought or word for the poor teacher left behind to her weary life. I thought I had got used to it, but you've been with me so long and uninterruptedly, that though you've given me more trouble than most, I've got attached to you somehow. I ought not to have got attached to you. It does not do for such as me to form attachments. You don't know how I shall miss you, left lonely here."

I looked at her, too astonished at this unexpected outburst to speak. Suddenly it struck me that the poor old thing did look very lonely, sitting by herself at the end of the long narrow table, in that bare room.

"I don't wonder you're glad to go," she went on, "my temper is sharp now, I know, and everything is very skimpy. I can't help it; I'm bound to be skimpy. The parents grind me down, your uncle has been no better than the rest of them, though he's a rich man. Do you think I wouldn't have things nice and pretty if I could, and have plenty on the table every day? Oh, I can tell you, Rosamund, for once you've gone hungry I've gone hungry twenty times——"

The sandwiches began to choke me, I could eat no longer.

—"And with all my skimping I get but little profit out of my school. If my health failed me, which it might do to-morrow, I shouldn't have enough to keep me three months out of the workhouse, and not a relation in the world to go to."

I sat aghast at the revelation. We had always understood, we girls, that Miss Skinner had saved a big bag of money by skimping us. "Have not you any money put by?" I asked.

"Not a penny. I had to keep my invalid brother for years, and it was a great drain upon me. I could not skimp him, he suffered so."

" Oh, Miss Skinner dear, I never knew! And is he dead?"

"He died five years ago; but for long before that he could not move about. He spent his days in that arm-chair in my room. He used to like that seat, because he could look out of the window and watch the flowers springing in my garden. Oh, I can see him now as he sat there for the last time, the day before he died. It was the early spring of the year. I was passing the door, and he called to me in such a pleased voice, 'Oh, Margaret, the crocuses are out, come and look at the crocuses'."

The poor thing broke down here, and began to sob in a manner pitiful to see in one her age. I began to sob also. I knew now why she sat so much in that arm-chair, looking sadly out upon her flower-beds. I knew now why she loved crocuses beyond every flower in the world. She no longer seemed the same woman. A halo of love and sorrow shone round her, and she was transfigured to my eyes. I left my seat, and rushed up to her and flung my arms passionately round her neck.

"Dear, dearest Miss Skinner," I said, "don't cry, Oh, don't cry. You shall never go to the workhouse, Felix will not allow it. And don't call yourself hard and unlovely, you are beautiful, quite beautiful! And I don't mind skimpiness, I love it, only I am sorry you should ever have gone hungry yourself. And your life has not been a mean life, it has been full of beauty, love first, now remembrance, and always flowers. And I am dreadfully sorry to leave you, more sorry than I can say. Dear Miss Skinner, do drink this wine, it will do you good, and eat these sandwiches, I really can't eat more. Please take them and look happier, or I shall go away miserable."

After a good deal more pressing Miss Skinner drank the wine, trying at the same time to hide her streaming eyes with the corner of the rusty black shawl covering her shoulders. The wine seemed to revive her, and gave her courage to attack the sandwiches, which she seemed really quite to enjoy. Poor thing, I am sure she needed them more than I did: I daresay her dinner had gone to make them.

"There's the cab!" she said presently. "I don't feel that I can come to see you off, Rosamund, I'm too upset, but cook will go with you, and will see to everything for you. Here's the money for your railway journey, five shillings for your ticket, and eighteenpence for the cab at this end, I've had directions to give you the exact sum, but I've added twopence of my own for the porter at Clapham Junction, where you change, because it is a bewildering station, and not being used to travelling you may want a little extra attention. Is Felix going to see you off at the station?—what was the note about?"

"He can't come," I said. "His grandmother made him go off with her to Berry Point."

Miss Skinner shook her head and gave a little groan. "Just as I expected," she said enigmatically, and then she rose and bade me farewell.

"Good-bye, Rosamund," she said in a shaky voice, "'twill be dreadfully strange and quiet without you. I can't think how my heart has twined so round you. But I hope you'll be happy in this new life you're going to. Think sometimes of old Miss Skinner, leading her weary life term after term, and year after year. Felix will look

after you, I don't think he will give you up.
Oh, Rosamund! you can't set too much store by
Felix.   He's a friend in a thousand.   I believe
now that you're truly fond of him, but for heaven's
sake don't spoil his life and your own by wild
ways and foolish tricks.   Remember, these
are my last words.   Now good-bye, and may
God bless you as He has not seen fit to bless
me. "

Somehow, through blinding tears, I left Miss
Skinner and entered the cab.   If anyone had
told me an hour before that my heart would ache
over the parting, I should not have believed
them; but it did ache sadly.

I never saw Miss Skinner again.   She was
spared the workhouse.   A year later she fell
asleep under her weary life, fell asleep suddenly,
in the spring time, just as another weary term
was beginning.   Fell asleep in her arm-chair, with
her face turned towards her little garden.   And

where she awoke we know not, but I like to
think that she awoke to find her narrow strip of
flower-beds had changed into a world of flowers,
and that her brother was there waiting for her
amidst the crocuses.

END OF BOOK I.

BOOK II.

MY PRISON HOUSE.

Book II.

CHAPTER I.

THE four years of school-life which I had dreaded so much had vanished; like a dream, like a bubble, like a bright exhalation in the evening, which no man sees more. For ten minutes I lay back in the railway carriage, sobbing because I had parted with Miss Skinner, and done with school for ever; then gradually school and Miss Skinner faded into air, into thin air. It was borne in upon me that we are indeed such stuff as dreams are made of. See! The insubstantial pageant fades and leaves not a rack behind. Gone is the skimpy home, and the little strip of flower-beds: before me dawns the great beautiful

world. Even the weeping lonely figure hiding
her streaming eyes behind the corner of her shawl
fades at last. The earth hath bubbles as the
water has, and Miss Skinner is of them. The
great globe itself claimed my attention now. It
whirled past me, dressed in all the trim of proud
pied April, a vision of green fields, shining
streams, and fruit trees glorified by masses of
pink and white blossom. Intensely interesting I
found it, yes, though lovely country disappeared
by degrees and merged itself in suburban town.
Even Clapham Junction had charms. The des-
perate, hurrying crowds, the trains shrieking by
like demons, filled me with excitement. This was
life, real life, and I was in the midst of it. Someone looked after me, and put me into the right
train for Wildacre : I have not the least idea
who he was, but he was kind and elderly and
respectable looking, and I offered him Miss Skinner's twopence when the bustle was over.

" For your extra attention," I said.

He stared at me, and he stared at the twopence, but he did not attempt to take it. And so I left him, my hand outstretched with twopence in it, and he staring after me and my departing train with an angry surprised expression upon his countenance.

The line was a little uninteresting after we had left Clapham. I could not decide whether I were passing through town or country, and the houses had a painful uniformity of ugliness. By degrees the people who had started with me got out at the different stopping-places, and I was left alone in the carriage. Another stop.

" *Wakcr!* " shouted a porter who was carelessly strolling down the platform. He sounded as if he had a cold in his head, but I have since discovered that most porters give you that disagreeable impression when they are shouting the names of places.

A great many people got out at Waker. I watched the bustle on the platform with much interest. One old man in particular interested me. He was the thinnest man I had ever seen, and carried his hat in his hand as he rushed excitedly up and down the platform, evidently hunting for someone, so I had the full benefit of his features. The face was a peculiar and yet an attractive one: very dark eyes and eyebrows contrasted well with white hair that stood erect on the forehead, somewhat after the manner of the crest of a cockatoo, and the complexion was so dark as to give him almost a foreign look. Suddenly his eyes fell upon me. He flew up to the carriage door with an alertness surprising in one whose hair was white with the snows of time.

"Where for, Madam?" he asked, poking a well-cut aquiline nose through the window.

"Wildacre," I answered.

"Of course. Here you are. Miss Gwynne, isn't it?"

"Yes, I'm Miss Gwynne," I answered, wondering how he could have known my name.

"I knew you were the instant my eyes fell upon your face," he exclaimed eagerly, and then he flung open the carriage door and apparently awaited my descent.

"I don't get out here," I remarked in surprise, "I'm for Wildacre."

"This is Wildacre, Madam."

"Oh, no, it's not," I said, "it's Waker."

"But I assure you, Madam, it is Wildacre, and I have come expressly to meet you."

I felt a little staggered, he seemed so positive, but just then catching sight of the porter with a cold in his head I shouted out to him:

"What station is this, porter?"

"Waker!" shouted back the porter, in precisely the same tone as before.

"There!" I exclaimed, "I told you it was Waker. You don't take *me* in, though I've never travelled before. Shut the door, please. I shall not get out here."

"But, Madam, I assure you the places are the same, precisely identical, exactly similar. You'll get no nearer by going further."

The poor old gentleman was getting so flustered, I could not refrain from a smile, but I had no intention of getting out at a wrong station at the bidding of a stranger, so I did not move. This seemed to drive him to desperation. He called the guard.

"Guard, please convince the young lady that this is Wildacre."

The guard examined my ticket, then convinced me it was Wildacre by bundling me out unceremoniously, and pointing afterwards to a signboard. "Wildacre" was written on it in huge characters, so at last I was forced to believe that Wildacre and Waker were the same.

And the stranger who had come to meet me must be my uncle, my unknown uncle! How ungracious I must have appeared. I turned upon him impetuously, anxious to make amends.

"I am so sorry I did not know you, uncle," I said, seizing his hands, and lifting my face to his for a kiss.

He shrank back looking quite appalled. "Oh, no, Madam, do not, I implore you, do not," he exclaimed affrightedly. "I have not the honour to be your uncle, I am only your uncle's er— er—confidential man, his servant in fact, Madam."

"Oh, indeed!" I said, "then my uncle is not like Julius Cæsar. You know what Julius Cæsar said—'Let me have men about me that are fat.'"

"Your uncle thinks differently. Have you any luggage, Madam?"

"He liked sleek-headed men, and such as sleep o' nights."

"Ticket, please," interrupted a porter.

I was far too interested in my subject to heed
him. "He objected to Cassius, you know, because
he had a lean and hungry look. He thought
thin men dangerous. I don't know that I quite
agree with him. I expect fat men are sometimes
to be avoided quite as much as thin men, but
Cæsar was perhaps justified in——"

The confidential man again interrupted me,
looking red and rather offended. "I may be thin,
Madam," he said, "but I hope I know my duty.
The porter has asked for your ticket twice, and
your luggage will be stolen unless we go and
look after it."

It was evident my remarks were not appreciated,
so I gave up my ticket and identified my luggage.
When we got out into the road I saw before
me a large, old-fashioned, double-seated carriage,
to which were harnessed a pair of grey horses.
On the box was a coachman in a rather faded
livery of brown. My box was lifted on to the

seat by the coachman, and then my escort held open the carriage door for me.

"Where are you going to sit?" I asked.

"Behind, Madam, in the dickey?"

"Is that the dickey, that dear little seat stuck on behind. Why, it's the nicest part of the carriage. I'll sit there with you, it will be so cosy."

"But, Madam, you really cannot sit behind in the dickey with me. You, a young lady, the master's niece, mistress of the whole establishment as you will be. It would create quite a scandal, Madam."

"Well, if you are really afraid of scandal, I won't sit there with you, but you must come and sit in the grand seats with me. I won't sit there alone with no one to talk to."

"But, Madam, that would be little better, my place is behind."

"Well, I'll sit with my back to the horses,

and you sit on the seat facing them, then we shall both be suited. I can talk, and you'll be a bit behind."

My companion gave a little groan. Finally it was arranged that he should sit with his back to the horses and I facing them, and then we started.

" What sort of a carriage do you call this? " I asked, as we drove up a hill between houses set in nice little gardens.

" A barouche, Madam; it has been in the family a great many years."

" So I should think; but I like it, it's so roomy. You can put your legs up."

" Yes, Madam, but it might be as well just to put your legs down until we are past the houses."

" Why? Scandal? "

"Well, it's unusual, Madam, a little unusual."

" Oh, well! I don't much care, I'll put them

down. Now tell me about my uncle. As you
are his confidential man I suppose you know
all about him. If he can afford such a nice
carriage, why did he stint me so, and grind
down poor Miss Skinner, and let me go without
any pocket-money?"

My companion looked quite distressed. "My
dear Madam, I never knew you were being
stinted, or I would not have allowed it to happen.
Oh, dear! What a pity you didn't write to me,
I would have sent you what you wanted at once."

I looked at him amazed. "I don't want your
money," I said.

"Not at all, Madam, of course not, it would
not have been my money. You cannot understand the situation yet, not knowing your uncle,
but I've been with him fifty-five years, ever since
he was a beautiful lad of ten, and I was the
same—in age, I mean—and I know how to manage
him, and how to get money from him when

it's wanted. But he's very troublesome. I've to keep my eye on him continually, or he stints somebody or something, and from first to last he's been very sly about you. I have often wondered how you were getting on. I am so vexed you should have been stinted. In future, when you want anything, I beg you will let me know, and it shall be obtained at once."

This sounded·very promising. I forgot Cæsar's prejudices, and began to think I should like this thin man. We had climbed the hill, and now the houses fell away before our approach, and in front of us opened a wide grassy plateau over which swept the most delicious breeze, and my familiar friends, the cloud shadows.

" Oh, what delicious air," I exclaimed. " Is this Wildacre Common? Oh, where is the castle?"

" This is the common. The castle lies some way further on, to the right of that windmill which you see defined against the sky."

"Is that a windmill! What a dear, sweet, picturesque old object. It is like a dark giant standing in a lonely land. See! it beckons with its arms, and the breeze comes rushing to refresh the world. I shall love this common. To whom does it belong?"

My companion lowered his voice as he answered me. "That is the great point, Madam. I wished to speak to you on the subject before you encountered your uncle. Don't be alarmed. The matter stands thus: as a matter of fact the common is free to everybody, to you or me, or any dog or cat, but your uncle—well he has a little mania on the subject, and he thinks it belongs to him, and that no one has a right to walk freely on it save by his permission."

"Why does he think it belongs to him?" I asked, beginning to think my uncle must be rather queer.

"Well, he's a bit mixed on the point, Madam.

Sometimes he says his ancestors enclosed it at the time of the Heptarchy and that it was approved afterwards under an old statute, and at others he says the god Woden took possession of this common, and left it to his family, and he thinks he's descended from the god Woden, so that's another claim, you see."

I began to feel uneasy. It was evident I was going to live with someone very peculiar.

"You will have to humour him on these points; I am afraid, Madam. Never contradict his statements, however absurd they may be. And please don't praise the Wildacre Common Act before him, it drives him wild. Say you never heard of it if he asks you, or else abuse it tremendously. You can praise up the old statute as much as you like, the statute of Merton in the time of Henry III. if you will try to remember, Madam."

"I shall be afraid to speak to him," I said, my spirits running rapidly down to zero.

"You need have no fear. Humour him on the subject of the common, and you'll find him a lamb, a perfect lamb. And in any difficulty come to me."

"But who are you? What is your name? Where do you come from?"

"My name is Matthew, Matthew Primavesi, at your service, Madam."

"What a strange surname! Is it foreign? Tell me more about yourself."

"My father was an Italian, his relations are unknown to me. He came to England and married my mother, nurse to your uncle afterwards. Two months after his marriage, my father died, killed by some machinery; none of her relations held out a helping hand to the poor widow, but your uncle's mother was a noble-hearted lady; I was born in her house, and your uncle and I grew up, so to speak, side by side. So you see, Madam, my own people were to me as though they existed not, and your uncle's people were everything to me. My life is now at your uncle's service, and I am most deeply attached to him. And, because you are his relation, I am at your service also."

"Thank you very much, Matthew. What is that house in front of us?"

"The castle, Madam."

"It's not a castle."

"No, Madam, but it's your uncle's whim to call it so."

It was not a castle, but it was a sweet old house, large, irregular, and covered with ivy like my old home in Wales. A balcony ran along the side next the windmill, a dear green balcony, garlanded with clinging plants not yet in flower, and connected with the ground by a flight of wooden steps which led down from the centre. All around the house was pleasant lawn shaded here and there by feathery silver birches, and just marked off from the common by a rustic wooden fence scarcely knee high. So unobtrusive was the fence, that, at a little distance, the eye did not perceive it, and private grounds seemed to merge indistinguishably into common, which added greatly to the charm of the place, giving it an indescribable air of sweet free wildness. The place had one curious feature. The middle of the house was higher than the rest, the roof was flat and square, and on the centre of it stood something which, as far as one could see from below, resembled a throne, or huge chair.

" What is that ?" I asked, pointing upwards. " It is difficult to distinguish it clearly from below."

" Valhalla, Madam," answered Matthew promptly. " Your uncle calls it Valhalla, it's just as well you should know. Every afternoon of his life he sits there with the Voluspa on his knee——"

This was a little too much for me. I had made up my mind to put up with a great deal, but I felt I could not stand Valhallas and Voluspas.

"Stop the carriage," I cried, jumping up excitedly. "I am going back, I won't enter that house to live with madmen and Voluspas. Let me get out."

"But, Madam, I assure you your uncle is quite harmless, a lamb, a perfect lamb," said Matthew hurriedly, trying at the same time to hold me back. "Oh, pray be seated again, there is nothing to fear. The Voluspa is only a book; don't leave the carriage, Madam, consider my position, sent to meet you, responsible for your safety. I assure you, your uncle is not a madman, in many ways he is as sane as I am."

"How do I know you are sane, perhaps you are mad too," I said, still striving to get out of the carriage.

Matthew sat down with a gesture of despair. "I'd rather give five pounds than go to meet a young lady again," he said, drawing out a red silk handkerchief and mopping his crest and forehead with it, "from first to last it's been a hard job to get you on."

There was something so very human and pathetic about him as he said this, that terror changed into pity as I looked at him. I sat down again, reflecting that I might as well give my new home a trial.

The carriage now drew up outside the little rustic fence, for within was no path or drive of any description. With Matthew's help I descended from the carriage, which then drove round to the back.

"This way, please, Madam," said Matthew, stepping over the fence and crossing the lawn towards the house. I followed closely, still somewhat uneasy.

"Well, Matthew, have you brought the Valkyrie?" cried a cheery voice.

Matthew drew aside, and waved me onwards towards the house, with a bow. Before me was an innocent-looking porch wreathed with leafy honeysuckle, and inside the porch was the plumpest, most affable-looking little gentleman I had ever seen in my life. He was really delightful to look at, so fresh his complexion, so white and curling his hair, so snowy his linen, so bland his smile. How could I have feared him even in anticipation? I rushed up to him with a feeling of intense relief, and giving him a warm embrace said: "Here I am, Uncle!"

He seemed surprised at my demonstrativeness, and drew back a little, but there was no sign of displeasure as he surveyed me; on the contrary his bland smile became if anything blander.

"Oh, here you are!" he said, "here you are, upon my word. Ha! no mistaking you, the true Scandinavian breed, fair face, free gestures, perfect outlines, golden hair. Really magnificent golden hair, isn't it, Matthew? I had no idea I was going to see such a fine specimen, quite a beautiful specimen. Why she'd have been a mate for Balder himself, Matthew. Come in, my dear, I am most pleased to see you, only don't destroy the sheets. How do you like my common?"

"I think it is perfect, windmill and all."

"Oh, but you've not seen the best part of it yet. I'll show you over to-morrow and we'll discuss some further improvements together. Matthew, show the Valkyrie upstairs. Just wash your hands and come down, my dear, no grand toilette necessary here, we just live in wild freedom on a common. But I don't like dinner kept waiting."

Matthew led me upstairs, and ushered me into a sweet little room, with a French window opening on to the balcony, and commanding a view of the windmill. Everything in the room looked light and fresh and pretty, from the painted ceiling to the flowery chintz and carpet.

"It's the prettiest room I have ever seen," I exclaimed delightedly. "How kind of uncle, I can see he's had it newly done up for me."

Matthew blushed a little. "Well, if I were you, I shouldn't mention the new things to your uncle, Madam, because the money is supposed to have gone in improving the common. We have to manage a little, to get money for household expenses, but I was determined you should have a pretty room."

So I had to thank Matthew, not my uncle. My heart warmed towards the kind, thoughtful creature, and his odd face grew more and more attractive to my eyes.

"Matthew," I said, "we shall be friends, I am sure. I should like you to be my confidential man as well as uncle's."

Matthew looked quite frightened. "There is a maid," he said hastily, "there is a housemaid who will attend to you in your room, and render you any little personal services you may require. I will send her to you. It will hardly do for me as a—er—as a—not feminine——"

"Oh, don't go on, I know; scandal!" I said laughingly, "you are very afraid of scandal. But of course I didn't mean that you were to mend my stockings and brush my hair. Why, Matthew, you *were* silly to think I meant that sort of thing!"

Matthew again blushed, recognizing his own folly, I suppose, and left the room.

CHAPTER II.

WE had quite a nice little dinner, my uncle and I; not for years had I eaten such a nice dinner. Matthew waited on us, and joined in the conversation when he felt inclined. We talked about the common a good deal, and I bore in mind Matthew's hints, and tried to avoid dangerous remarks. All went well until the interval before cheese. Then my uncle asked me suddenly if I was aware that he was an impoverished man.

"I don't think you can be very impoverished," I said laughingly; a not unnatural answer, seeing that at the moment I was surrounded by every luxury.

"You doubt my poverty then?" he said, an excited look coming into his blue eyes.

Matthew made some violent signs and grimaces, which I rightly interpreted to mean I was not to doubt my uncle's poverty, but a little indignation arose in my breast, and triumphed over diplomacy. I considered my uncle had behaved very meanly to me whilst I was at school: I had thought so from the moment my eyes fell upon his fine carriage and horses, and the evidences of his wealth which met me at every turn, increased the feeling. He had ground down poor weary, overworked Miss Skinner, but he could afford a beautifully furnished house, and a well-appointed table. And now he was trying to excuse himself on the score of poverty! I was not going to stand it.

"Yes, I do," I answered firmly.

"But I tell you it is true. I am a poor man. Now do you doubt it?"

Matthew made more signs and grimaces, but I answered doggedly: "Certainly I doubt it."

"You hear her, Matthew! She doubts my poverty! No, thank you, no cheese, nothing more. I shall go upstairs. I will not stay here with her." He rose in an agitated manner from the table. His face was crimson, his smile had vanished.

Seeing how disturbed he was I began to feel sorry I had expressed my doubt. We had been so cheery together before, it seemed a pity to have displaced the mirth, broke the good meeting.

"Oh, please, don't go away, uncle," I cried repentantly. "I am quite willing to believe you are an impoverished man, since you tell me so. I always did believe it at school. I felt sure you would have sent me pocket-money had it been otherwise."

My uncle sat down again after this apology, but his spirits did not revive immediately. He remarked that his appetite had gone, and buried his face in his hands, looking exceedingly low. Matthew at this juncture was a marvel. He hovered over his master like an eagle ministering to its young, offering him tempting fruits, and saying everything he could think of as likely to raise the spirits of an impoverished man.

"Yes, you are poor, very poor," he said at length, darting to the sideboard and fetching thence a decanter, "but you have kind and grateful friends for all that. Here!"—putting down the decanter on the table with a flourish—"here is a bottle of '47 port, most beautiful '47 port."

My uncle raised his head quickly with a dawning smile. "Eh? '47 port? Where did that come from?"

"Sent this morning, Sir," said Matthew, without a shadow of hesitation. "Sent by the invalid lady with best thanks to you for so kindly allowing her to come on the common with her donkey and bath-chair yesterday."

"Oh, indeed! very proper of her, very proper feeling indeed. Tell her she may come again to-morrow. It's beautiful port! I feel better, my appetite has returned, I'll take some of those grapes. Ha! This is nice and pleasant. Good wine, agreeable company. Take a chair, Matthew, draw it up by me, opposite the Valkyrie. I want to explain how it is I am so impoverished."

Matthew drew a chair up to the table and sat down in an apologetic attitude, on the very edge of it.

"Have you heard of the Wildacre Common Act?" asked my uncle, turning sharply upon me.

"Yes—no—yes," I answered confusedly, feeling rather flustered by the nods and signs Matthew was making opposite me.

"Yes, d'you mean, yes? Oh! all right, yes! You've heard about it. Iniquitous, isn't it?"

"Abominable!" I answered, taking my cue better this time.

"Shameful!" said Matthew.

"It made over my common, *my* common, mind you, to a body of conservators! Did you ever hear of such a thing? Conservators for my common! People resident in this neighbourhood whom I have never visited, would not condescend to visit. People, many of them, with absolutely no pedigree, and mine goes back to the god Woden. Now isn't that iniquitous?"

"Abominable!" I said again.

"Shameful," repeated Matthew.

"It has been my common since time immemorial; mine by a double right. Mine by birthright, for the god Woden once used it as a pasture land for all superfluous animals; and mine by right of law, for our annexation of it in the early days of the Heptarchy was approved in the reign of our most gracious sovereign Henry III. under the Statute of Merton. You've heard of the Statute of Merton, of course? Good old statute, isn't it?"

"Oh, magnificent!" I said.

"A grand old statute," remarked Matthew.

"Quite so," said my uncle, beaming benevolently upon us. "Take a glass of port, both of you. Now you understand how the common came to be mine. Well, now, would you believe it, this iniquitous Act I was speaking of—the Wildacre Common Act— not only made over my common to a body of conservators, but also laid down that an upstart personage called the Lord of the Manor, who used to cut down my trees and dig out my gravel, was to receive an annuity on condition he abstained from digging and cutting! Was to be paid, in fact, for not thieving! Now do you understand the full monstrosity of the Act?"

We murmured, "shameful", and "abominable", as a token that we did.

"Well, I pay that annuity. Parliament has decreed that it shall be paid, and I don't like to go against the government of my country. No!

I'd rather impoverish myself. I pay the Lord of the Manor, I pay him for not thieving, I support him, he lives on my charity. I pay the man weekly, send him so many pounds a week by my confidential man here, Matthew. Good plan that, paying him by the week, isn't it? Matthew suggested it."

"A splendid plan," I answered, beginning to understand how Matthew managed to get funds for household expenses. Our nice little dinner would be paid for out of the Lord of the Manor's annuity.

"Of course it is a great drain on my resources disbursing such a sum every week, it impoverishes me sadly; and I have other serious calls upon my purse. My claim is universally recognized by the people living around me. The conservators refuse to act except under my orders. They send to consult me, through Matthew here, before they dare to cut down a single tree. *I* decide whether a path is wanted or not, whether a piece of wood wants thinning, whether a seat should be made here, or a pond there. To me the inhabitants around come for permission to walk about on the common. And all the expenses of managing the open space are charged upon me. That is only fair. I must accept the responsibilities of my position as owner of a common five thousand acres in extent."

He paused here, and looked at me as though expecting me to say something. I racked my brains for something appropriate to say, and finally asked nervously if the Lord of the Manor were a nice man.

"A nice man!" cried my uncle, helping himself excitedly to a third glass of port—"How can an able-bodied man who accepts charity once a week be a nice man? Are thieves usually nice men? Nice, indeed! I'll tell you where he's very likely to go—he'll go to Niflheim!"

" Where is Niflheim ?" I inquired.

" Ha! Ha! hear her, Matthew! She asks where Niflheim is. Ha! Ha! she doesn't know where Niflheim is !"

" It's a very bad place, Madam," said Matthew kindly.

" Ha! Ha! Yes, a very bad place, a very cold place, icily cold, freezingly cold," went on my uncle, roaring with laughter in a most peculiar way, and rolling about on his seat until he nearly fell on the floor.

I looked at him half alarmed, and began suddenly to feel very tired.

Matthew got up, and quietly removed the port, locking it up in the sideboard and pocketing the keys.

" Time for your nap, Sir," he then said, addressing my uncle in a very firm voice.

" So it is. I feel quite sleepy, now you remind me of it. My dear, don't remain with the gentle-

men any longer than you feel inclined. It is
my custom to take a nap after dinner on this
sofa, but there are two charming sitting-rooms
at your disposal. Good-night, my dear. Matthew
will show you the rooms. I hope you won't destroy the sheets."

I assured him I no longer destroyed sheets,
then, remembering how he had drawn back from
my first embrace, shook hands with him and followed Matthew out of the room.

The sitting-rooms were charming, especially
one which faced the west and was lined with
books. I selected that to sit in, and Matthew
brought me in a lamp, and left me there, hoping
I should be able to amuse myself with the
books. When he had gone I took down a
large volume of Shakspere, and for a time the
beautiful illustrations by Kenny Meadows gave
me great delight. Then I began to feel lonely,
and a vision of my uncle lying asleep with a

horrible smile upon his face began to haunt me.
I longed for Felix. Though 'twas but a day since
we had parted, I felt as if it were years. I
had been for so long accustomed to have him near,
and now he seemed so very far away, almost
lost to me. How quiet the house was, unnatu-
rally quiet; Miss Skinner's harsh voice breaking in
upon the stillness would have been a positive joy.
I wondered if I should ever hear it again, or the
girlish laughs of my companions-of-the-bedchamber? When people passed from one phase of life
to another, did the past life utterly vanish, and
become an irrevocably lost thing, of which no
part, or actor in it, could ever be recalled? Was
that the way of life? It almost seemed so. Had
not my childhood's home in Wales utterly
vanished, and everyone who had taken part in
it become dead to me? Now, sitting here alone,
in this strange house, was I irrevocably lost to all
who had known and loved me in my school-

life? A little sob arose in my throat, as I thought of it. Impossible to sit here any longer, I resolved to go to bed. No one was about as I passed through the hall, and the stairs and passages were silent and deserted. The house might have been empty, it was so still.

The whole place seemed penetrated with my uncle's sleep. In my room a little silver lamp was burning, and everything was ready for the night, but the silence and the loneliness of the house seemed to have crept in even there. I unlatched the window, and stepped out upon the balcony. The silence and loneliness were there too. Everything was steeped in a dreadful sleep. The windmill looked weird and ghostly against the dark sky, full of some dread significance I could not understand. Its arms pointed warningly over the common, which lay all around, shadowy in the foreground, impenetrably black beyond. Nowhere was there any light.

Suddenly a black figure darted into view and came to a standstill at the bottom of the wooden steps which led down from where I stood. It startled me horribly, and I gave a terrified cry.

"Madam, Madam, it is I," said the voice of Matthew. "I came round to see if all was safe, and never thought to frighten you, or find you here."

"Come up, Matthew, come up," I cried, trembling all over. "I feel so lonely, oh, so lonely! I don't think I am going to be happy here at all. I don't think I can stay here, I am so frightened."

"Don't be frightened, my dear, take my word for it, there is nothing to fear," he said soothingly, mounting the steps to my side.

"Matthew, my uncle is mad. It is of no use your denying it any longer."

"Well, Madam, as you have perceived it, I suppose it is of no use denying that his mind is a little warped on some points, but then he can be managed, so it comes to much the same thing in the end as if he were sane. And indeed, Madam, if you knew the world as well as I do, you'd find there were heaps of people as mad as he, and madder, who are thought mighty clever by their fellow-creatures. It's by no means the maddest that are clapped into lunatic asylums, I can tell you. It is very difficult nowadays to distinguish the sane from the insane. Please believe me, Madam, when I say, from your uncle you have nothing to fear. I really do think that if you can—accommodate yourself to circumstances, you will find it a pleasant home. It is a strange place for a young lady, I admit; for many reasons I am sorry there is no other home open to you; but there is nothing to fear."

"Matthew, did—did my mother know he was mad?"

"No, my dear," answered Matthew, with a deep sigh, "and that's where the mistake was made. Had she known she'd have left you to another guardian perhaps. But for poor master's sake, it has always been kept very quiet, and he having no relations except the one sister Frances who married early, and never saw much of her brother afterwards, it was easy to keep the sad truth from your mother's ear. I don't think your mother saw the poor master but once, and then she was a child, too young to understand, if he was a bit peculiar. And so, not knowing, on her deathbed she wrote and committed you to his care; there was no one else to look after you, and the thing was done. A year or two ago your father seemed inclined to interfere and claim you—but——"

"But what, Matthew? How was I saved?"

" You don't know?"

" Don't know what?"

" What happened to your poor father?"

"No, and I don't feel as if I much cared," I answered fiercely.

" Hush! my dear. Speak gently of one whose life on earth is over, and whose faults have now to be dealt with by other hands than ours."

" Do you mean that he is dead ? " I whispered.

" Yes, dead. He died two years ago, after a terrible illness during which he was deserted by the one for whom he had given up wife and child and home. Died alone, in a foreign land, with no friend near to soothe the last dark hours."

I sat mute, shocked beyond measure. No hard thoughts were possible now. Far, far away I seemed to see that lonely, miserable deathbed: sadder did it seem for a moment, even than my mother's weeping. He who was dead had been but a name to me, but that name was—father.

"I feel very alone in the world, Matthew," I said, a choking feeling rising in my throat."

" Yes, poor dear. But I'll see you are taken care of and come to no harm. Let me try and explain my position here. I am a servant, and the son of a servant, I never forget that, or the respect due from me to your family. I never forget my place. Still I am in authority here. Your uncle is living on his mother's money left to him by will, and she left him to my care, and appointed me executor, knowing there was no one in the world so attached to him as I, or so anxious to save him from the worst horrors of his terrible affliction. So you see, Madam, though a servant, I occupy a position of authority and trust. And after your uncle's death his money —but time enough for you to know all that again. Your uncle, though your *great*-uncle, is still well and strong, and young for his sixty-five years."

"You said, Matthew, that my mother wrote to my uncle committing me to his care. How I should love to see, to have, that letter. Her last letter, written on her deathbed, about me!"

"You shall," said Matthew. "I know where it is, and will get it for you."

He darted away, leaving me alone on the
balcony.   In a few moments he darted back again,
a letter in his hand.   I took it from him silently,
and sat down to read it on the ground by the
open window, just where the light streamed from
the silver lamp.   The writing was strange to me,
the paper was crumpled, the ink faded: it was
altogether the letter of a person hopelessly far
away, irretrievably gone.

"Dear Uncle Lawrence,

"I am dying, and my little girl, my only
one, will be left without a protector.   Uncle, take
care of the little darling that I must leave.   Send
her to some good school where she will be happy, if
you feel you cannot receive a child; look after
her and give her a home when she is a woman.
For the love of God I entreat you to do this
for me.   Be good to the little one, left mother-
less and worse than fatherless.   I am too weak

to write more, but they will tell you when the end comes.

"FRANCES."

I read it through, and then suddenly I burst into dreadful weeping. Matthew looked at me helplessly, entreating me not to weep, but the fit had to have its way; I could not still my sobs though they seemed to tear me in two. At length the paroxysm passed, and I became quiet again.

"I am so sorry, Matthew," I said, "but reading that was like hearing her dead voice. She was my loved one. I was her little girl, her only one. Oh, I am crying again! I can't stop! I think I am ill, I don't know what is the matter with me."

"You are tired, poor dear, your journey has tired you, and everything has been strange. You are over-excited, you are nervous, you are un-strung, I could see it by your face at dinner.

It is rather a strain on the nerves to be a long time in the master's company, don't I know it, I, who am with him day and night? It's that has taken all the flesh off my bones. But don't you fret yourself about anything, poor little dear; Matthew will take care of you, Matthew will see you have everything you can possibly desire."

"But you are old, Matthew, suppose you died, I could never manage my uncle alone."

"Leave that to God, Madam. He will take care of you, God will take care of you."

His words soothed me. The darkness seemed to grow more friendly, the vague cloud of terror lifted. I lost my fear of the uncle sleeping below, and went to bed, with the loved one's letter under my pillow. And in the middle of the night I dreamed that my window flew suddenly open, and that someone came and stood there in the opening, saying,—"God

will take care of you."—And in my dream
I looked up, and behold! it was Matthew
who stood there. But he had become an angel,
with great wings that streamed far out into the
night.

CHAPTER III.

SUCH a bright beautiful morning! It seemed absurd to think that darkness and loneliness could have frightened me only a few hours ago. I rose, dressed, and ran down the balcony steps on to the common to refresh myself in the morn and liquid dew. My spirits rose as I ran across the spangled turf. On and on I sped, until the windmill was left behind, and the ground began to be dotted with ever thickening bracken and furze. So thick it grew, that at last I could scarcely wade through it, but I persevered, for my goal was a wood I saw on the slope beyond. The wood gained, I found myself at the entrance

212

of a beautiful glade, where the branches met overhead, forming a dewy green arcade alive with the voices of innumerable birds. Down the arcade I wandered, longing for the companionship of the one I loved best. I found it was but one of many green arcades, they opened out to right and left of me, these branching off again into others, forming a network in which the unwary stroller might easily lose his way. Fearful of losing myself I retraced my steps before I had penetrated far, resolving to bring Felix as a guide, at the earliest opportunity. Little did I think then that it would not be with Felix I should wander down the green arcades, but with another.

The sun was high and bright by this time. It drank the dew from off my skirts as I walked home along the springy turf, and made the gorse blossoms shine before my eyes like brightest gold. In the porch Matthew and my uncle were waiting for me, the latter all smile and spotlessness. I ran up to him and bade him good morning brightly, feeling that even if he were a little mad, it was not of much consequence, life, with sunshine in it, could always be made delightful.

My uncle seemed pleased with my cheeriness, and remarked to Matthew as we entered the dining-room that now he had seen me he didn't so much mind maintaining me.

"Sit there, at the head of the table, my dear," he said to me pleasantly. "Excuse my having a separate teapot for myself. I know it is a lady's province to pour out tea for gentlemen, but I like to put my milk and sugar in the teapot and sip my tea comfortably from the spout. People don't seem to know it, but it is by far the most sensible way of taking tea. Not only does the tea keep hotter than when poured out, but it grows stronger as you progress with your meal. No wishy-washy third cup my way."

Now was it mad to drink from the spout or was it not? I could not make up my mind; the question puzzled me throughout breakfast. It looked peculiar, of course, but it really did seem sensible now he had explained his reasons. Matthew must have been right in what he had said; it certainly was very difficult to distinguish the sane from the insane. Could it be that insanity was merely a different way of looking at things from the usual way, and if so why should not the insane be as sane as the sane? My brain grew so muddled over the question I gave it up at last, and finished my tea out of the spout to see how it tasted. It was exceedingly nice.

When breakfast was over my uncle turned to me and said: "My dear, as you are aware, you are my niece."

"Yes, uncle Lawrence," I replied, in my best schoolroom manner.

"You are my niece, dependent upon me. Of

course you are aware you are penniless. Your
father chose to squander all his money away on
that crea——"

Here Matthew gave him a nudge, and he
stopped abruptly.

"Oh, well!" he went on after a moment, "to
do him justice he kept up his remittances to your
poor mother until she died. But what was I
saying—Oh! you are dependent upon me, and
penniless. Nevertheless my dear, as my niece,
your position is one of great dignity. I quite
recognize it, and I wish you to understand that
you are mistress here. Do as you like, go where
you like, behave as you like, only be punctual
at meals, and don't on any account attempt to
associate with your neighbours. They are none
of them your equals, and I intend to be very
particular on that point. Do you understand me?"

I replied that I did, feeling very flat at the
idea of being debarred from all society.

"Well and good. That is all I ask of you. Consider yourself from this moment mistress of my establishment. Matthew, behold your future mistress."

Matthew bowed.

Your mistress will now order dinner, Matthew. I will leave you together so as to be no check upon you."

He left the room and partly closed the door after him, but I could see, though Matthew could not, that he was listening behind the chink he had left open.

I looked at Matthew. He stood before me, silently awaiting my orders.

"Well, Matthew?" I said.

"At your service, Madam."

"What about dinner?"

"Would you like to see the cook, Madam?"

"Oh, dear no, thank you. Better not, I think, because I don't know in the least what to say to her."

"Very well, Madam, then I will take your orders."

"Very well, Matthew, and what do you think they'd better be?"

"Well, to begin with, what do you say to some oxtail soup? we've got a nice tail in the house."

The door was flung open and my uncle burst violently into the room. "Where did that tail come from, Matthew? How came you by that tail? You don't mean to say that, knowing my poverty, you bought that tail?"

For a moment Matthew was taken by surprise, but he quickly recovered himself.

"Some boys brought it this morning, Sir, with their best respects, and might they throw sticks into your pond, and would you allow their dogs to go into the water after them?"

"Oh, certainly!" replied my uncle, immediately mollified by this explanation. "Tell them to bring their dogs to play in the pond as often as they please. Don't let me disturb you, continue your orders, my dear."

He left the room again, but I could still see him listening behind the door, so kicked Matthew quietly to let him know it.

"Then, Madam, I would suggest a leg of lamb sent by the riding-master with his best respects to my master, and he and the young ladies greatly enjoyed their gallop over master's common yesterday. There is some nice asparagus too, left at the door by a baby's mother with many apologies for taking the perambulator over the turf, and some nice rhubarb from the green-grocer, who feels he trespasses on master's kindness by using the roads on the common so often, and a cream cheese from the postman who feels the same. I think that is all in the house for to-day, Madam."

"Very good indeed. I think it's a splendid dinner. We didn't get dinners like that at Miss

Skinner's. Those are my orders. Oh! I'm very fond of jelly if anyone leaves some."

Here I gave another surreptitious kick, and I saw by Matthew's expression that he understood it, and that someone would leave that jelly before dinner time.

"Ah! Finished?" asked my uncle sauntering blandly in at this juncture. "I hope it has not fatigued you, my idea. Luncheon requires no ordering because I make a rule of finishing up the remains of yesterday's dinner Now, Matthew, get through your morning duties as quickly as possible, because I want to take the Valkyrie for a stroll on the common."

Matthew left the room. As soon as he was out of hearing my uncle said with an evidently forced attempt at carelessness—"By the bye, my dear, don't say much before Matthew about the manners and customs of your late home. I daresay the dinners weren't very good there, but economy must be studied, that's what I never can get Matthew to understand. He's a very good fellow, but"—here my uncle tapped his forehead significantly--"a little peculiar you know, and he was inclined to be suspicious about that school."

I longed to say, "You mean, you were sly about it," but diplomacy prevailed this time, and I didn't. It struck me as curious that my uncle should think Matthew insane, it showed he was unconscious of his own insanity, and made the problem of madness more confusing to me than ever.

Half an hour later we met in the porch for our walk, my uncle in a smart white sailor hat and I in my bulged black one. Matthew sported a quiet black felt, probably to mark the difference in his station. He would not have presumed to wear a sailor hat like us. Unobtrusive though as he was in attire and general bearing, his dark foreign face and strikingly white hair had a charm of their own, and gave him very much the air of a gentleman.

There is no air in the world like that which
blows over Wildacre Common. Nimbly and
sweetly it recommends itself unto our gentle
senses. It floats over the open land, laden with
the sweet breath of gorse and clover, of turf and
spicy wood. Fresh and pure it sweeps along,
whispering to us that we have wandered into
untainted country, millions and millions of miles
away from London, and so persuasive is the
ambient whisper, fain are we to believe.

We had a very pleasant walk, or perhaps it
would be more correct to say prowl, for my
uncle did not seem to want to go in any particular direction, and followed no course long.
Still it was a very pleasant prowl. A slight
haze lay over the level land to east and north,
giving a great effect of distance, and making it
seem like an almost boundless prairie, whilst to
the west, the ground fell away in copse-clad slopes
and dingles, growing ever more and more sylvan

in character, until at length it swelled and rose again in exquisitely wooded hills, glorified by the sunshine, and tenderly green from the hand of Spring.

I noticed that Matthew did not seem to enjoy his walk as much as his master and I did. He wore an anxious air, and kept very close to my uncle if ever a person approached us, talking very fast as though to divert his master's attention from the passer-by, and hurrying him on as much as possible.

Fortunately, pedestrians on this part of the common were few and far between, but once when a man came very near us, my uncle muttered an angry oath, and showed a decided intention to stop and address him. The stranger paused for a second in surprise, seeing he was about to be accosted.

"Just you come on, Sir," said Matthew, touching my uncle on the arm, and speaking in a low but determined tone, "you can't prosecute this gentleman."

The stranger passed on, with a stare of surprise. My uncle looked after him angrily.

"Why not?" he asked, in a fierce tone, "why should he not be prosecuted? He's trespassing on my private grounds."

"He asked permission, Sir, and he provided you with strawberries all last summer."

" Well, d——n it, Matthew, let me thank the fellow."

"Certainly not, Sir, you a descendant of the god Woden, thank a man personally for a few strawberries. Most undignified, Sir."

Very unwillingly my uncle moved on, still casting hankering looks after the stranger. He had given in to the stronger will, but I could see he had got into a great state of irritation. By an unfortunate chance, immediately after this contretemps a cat appeared on the common, frisking about quite as if he knew the five thousand acres were public property. I could see by my uncle's face that he regarded each caper as a deliberate insult, his face grew redder and redder, and he shouted to the impertinent animal again and again. Finally he said he should chase the creature, and wring its neck until every purr was out of it for ever. In vain did Matthew try to dissuade him, the cat could not possibly be supposed to have sent strawberries or viands of any description, and there was really no excuse to make for its conduct. Off went my uncle after it, his coat tails flying in the breeze, and his straw hat dangling half way down his back by a string. He ran and he ran, but he could not succeed in catching the cat, for that intelligent creature soon became a bounding speck in the far distance. We hurried after its pursuer and succeeded in catching him up soon after the chase was over.

"That's the eighth time I've caught the villain trespassing," cried my uncle, angrily mopping his forehead.

"You'd best leave him alone, Sir," said Matthew, looking somewhat weary. "You'll never catch him. If I were you I'd give that cat a free pass over the common."

But my uncle scouted the idea of giving any cat a free pass over his common. Indeed, so angry did the mere suggestion make him that he refused to walk home with us, but loitered behind in sulky silence, and it took two glasses of '47 port and Matthew's choicest blandishments to restore him to good humour and his smile.

It would be tedious to recount to you in detail the experiences of my first days at "the castle." I have already related enough to give you an idea of the life which opened before me. In the morning I invariably rose early and had a run on the common, returning to breakfast, and tea out of the spout of a teapot. Afterwards I ordered dinner, whilst my uncle listened behind the door to find out if we were being economical, and Matthew accounted for the provisions with inexhaustible ingenuity.

Afterwards we went for a prowl on the common, which was always diverting to me by reason of my uncle's vagaries, but which seemed to try Matthew's nerves more than any part of the day. For, as he said, if my uncle were allowed to annoy the inhabitants, they might object to his enjoying so much freedom; indeed, it might become necessary to keep him under much closer restraint. Therefore every effort must be made to guard against such a contingency, and when he took his daily walk he must be watched and guarded with unceasing vigilance. Naturally this did involve some strain, and always, after the morning walk, Matthew looked weary. I no longer wondered he was so thin. But he would have worn himself to the very bone sooner than deprive his dear master of his daily outing.

After luncheon my uncle always went up to "Valhalla" with a great book under his arm, and there, when fine, he spent the whole afternoon. But he was very reticent about his afternoon pursuits, and I was never allowed to peep into the book or set foot on Valhalla. Fortunately the shelves of the room facing the west provided me with plenty of nice reading, and in that room, which I christened "the library," I generally passed the afternoon. Matthew always brought me a prettily served tea at five o'clock, and chatted with me whilst I drank it. We talked a great deal of Miss Skinner and her school, and sometimes we discussed uncle Lawrence and his peculiarities, but for some time I breathed no word of Felix, though he was in my thoughts by night and by day.

In spite of the monotony of the life, it was

some time before I began to feel dull. My uncle's vagaries gave an element of strangeness and excitement to the monotony, and afforded matter for endless speculation. No one ever knew what he would say or do next, or when he would take offence, and though he had fallen into certain habits of life, there was always a feeling that at any moment he might depart from them.

I soon lost all personal fear of him, but could not get quite used to his incomprehensible, irresponsible individuality, and always felt it was a strain to be long in his company. His conversation wearied and bewildered me. As a rule the thread of his verbosity was finer than the staple of his argument, but sometimes he was so clear and logical that I used to feel quite startled, and wonder whether after all it could be that he was sane, and Matthew and I and the rest of the world insane.

A question of such paramount importance could not, of course, be easily dismissed from my mind. To find out if it could be so I used to try and put myself in my uncle's place, and look at things from his point of view. This was hard work. I had first of all to consider the world at large as mistaken and insane in its ideas; then, to imagine myself a madman and reason as I thought a madman would reason; and, finally, to decide whether this reasoning could be considered sane. Half-an-hour's effort of this kind would make me hot all over, and at length in despair I came to the conclusion that between sanity and insanity there was no marked line, and that we all wavered between the two.

It was not a healthy atmosphere for a young girl. I had absolutely no society beyond that of my uncle and Matthew. The cook and house-maid were uninteresting unintelligent women, who rarely came in contact with the high life upstairs.

Matthew had them entirely under his control, and took great and evident care to keep them apart from us as much as possible, feeling, no doubt, that the less they saw of their master the more likely they would be to remain with him. It was suggested at the beginning that the house-maid should act as lady's-maid to me, but I soon dispensed with her services at my toilette, for she had a puffing, panting way with her, which was very disagreeable.

One or two ladies kindly called upon me in the course of the second week, but they were not admitted, and my uncle was extremely an-gered by their presumption. He said it was gross impertinence on their parts to call upon descend-ants of the god Woden, and he ground their cards into a pulp with the dining-room poker. It was after this that I began to feel dull. I did not care especially about knowing the first lady, for I peeped over the balustrade when Matthew answered the door, and saw she was plain and elderly, but when the second lady called I peeped again, and I saw she had with her a young girl of my own age, a nice, pretty, dear-looking young girl whom it would have delighted me to know. My spirits went down to zero when she was sent away, I did so yearn for a young companion. It was dreadful to learn that I was to be cut off from all society. I felt as if I could not endure such a hermit life.

My thoughts from the first had been much with Felix, now I began absolutely to pine for him. He had said he would come soon, but day after day passed and he came not. Neither did he write. I dared not write to him for he had especially begged me to address no letters to his grandmother's house, so I was left entirely without news of him. It fretted me sorely, this silence and delay, for it was not like Felix to keep me in suspense. Was he going to melt into air, into thin air, like Miss Skinner and her little strip of flower-beds, and my lost companions-of-the-bedchamber. Was I never again to see that best-loved face which had brightened the sordid, skimpy school-life? This dreadful fear so pressed upon me that I began to lose both my spirits and my appetite. Matthew's eagle eye was not long in discovering this.

"You are low, Madam, you are very low," he said one afternoon, depositing the tea-tray on a little table by my side, as I lay curled up on the sofa. "There are traces of tears on your eyelashes: tell Matthew what ails you. Matthew is your friend, there is nothing you can desire that he will not get for you if it lies in his power."

I looked up at him as he bent over me, a hand on either side the tea-tray. As I looked, I felt instinctively that Matthew had a beautiful soul. It shone through him; it showed in his

face, illumined by pure, unselfish, anxious tenderness, even in his very hands, tense in their
desire to do me service. I felt I could open my
heart to the devoted creature.

"Matthew!" I cried, rising into a sitting posture
and speaking very tragically, "I am undone."

Perhaps I spoke more tragically than the occasion
demanded, for Matthew looked quite frightened.

"Yes," I said, feeling rather pleased at the
effect I had produced. "Undone. There is
no living, none, if Felix be away. Matthew, if
you have tears, prepare to shed them now. We
were torn from one another's arms, and I have
been here nearly three weeks, yet he has never
come to see me as he promised, nor written.
My heart is cold with despair, 'tis getting like
the frosty Caucasus."

"Oh, dear! Oh, dear! This is very sad!" said
Matthew, looking immensely concerned.

His sympathy comforted me, and I began to

feel a certain pleasure in relating my tale of sorrow. "We were like twin lambs that freak'd i' the sun," I went on, rising to the occasion, and growing more and more dramatic, "twin lambs that bleated the one at the other."

"Dear, dear! How very sad!" said Matthew, again, still bending over me with a hand on either side the tea-tray.

"Together each morn we woke Diana with a hymn, and at eve we were still quiring, to the young-eyed cherubins."

Matthew looked puzzled. "He is a good harmlessly-disposèd young man then?" he inquired anxiously.

"Eminently so," I answered.

Matthew looked much impressed. "And may I ask if he is very handsome, Madam?" he inquired respectfully.

"Handsome! His person beggars all description—Imagine Hyperion's curls——"

"Oh, Madam, Madam!" cried Matthew, interrupting me ruthlessly, "don't wave the teapot about so, the tea is jerking out all over the carpet."

Thus swiftly brought down from the sublime to the ridiculous, I put down the teapot with which I had been unconsciously emphasizing my words, and rather pettishly told Matthew to pour out the tea for me himself. I think he was sorry to have checked me in my confidences, for he began fussing nervously over the cakes and cream, and begged me to tell him more about my friend. It was a nice, daintily served tea, but I felt too low to do justice to it, and all inclination to rhapsodize further about Felix had gone.

"Can nothing be done?" asked Matthew, evidently much distressed by my heavy sighs and want of appetite. "Can't I fetch Mr. Felix from somewhere?"

"No. I won't have him fetched. It would be quite beneath my dignity as mistress of this establishment. He can stay away if he does not want to come. I'm sure I don't care, it is more his loss than mine——" Here I broke off, bent my head over the tray, and began to sob bitterly into my tea-cup.

Matthew looked distracted. "O Madam, O poor young thing, don't cry," he exclaimed. "You are flushing your dear pretty face so, and the beautiful gold curls are all going into the cream jug. Oh, dear! If I could only have let those ladies in! Mothers of families both of them, who called in pure kindness of heart, seeing you run about so wild and lonely with no one but stupid old Matthew to look after you. It's what you want, nice female friends to advise you, and take the place of a mother to you."

"Yes, it's what I want," I said, sobbing more bitterly than ever.

"Was your late instructress acquainted with Mr. Felix, Madam?"

"Yes, he lived next door," I answered between my sobs—"and—she was very fond of him."

"Why not write to her and make inquiries?"

"She won't answer. She will always be very pleased to hear from me, but I must not expect to hear from her, except at Christmas time, stamps are such a consideration."

"Stamps are no consideration. She shall be sent a dozen, two dozen, we'll write at once and enclose them, and Mr. Felix shall be found and brought here. That's right, my dear, stop crying; remember your dignity as mistress of this establishment. Here we are now, paper, pen, ink, stamps, more stamps, heaps of stamps! Come to this writing-table; now write and inquire, say we are quite surprised at Mr. Felix, that we think his silence quite unpardonable."

"Writing to inquire won't sound as if I wanted him very badly, and he didn't want to come, will it?" I asked.

" Certainly not. A queen might send to inquire after a subject, the course is a most dignified one."

Thus assured, I dried my eyes, sat down to the writing-table, and began to compose a letter to Miss Skinner, whilst Matthew stood by me, wiping the cream off my curls and offering suggestions. The letter was very dignified at the beginning, but it became very much less so towards the end, Matthew and I both grew so excited over it; and when it was finished somehow we found ourselves composing one to Felix, to be enclosed in the one to Miss Skinner. We had warmed to our work by this time, and the second letter was one calculated to bring a ghost out of his grave. I felt it could not fail to tear Felix's heart and bring him bounding over walls and precipices to my side, if once it fell into his hands. Then we enclosed two dozen stamps for a reply, sealed the letter with a huge seal so that no one could tamper with it, and paused to take breath again.

Matthew took the letter to the post himself. I watched for his return from an upper bedroom window, and by arrangement he waved his handkerchief the whole way home across the common, so that as soon as he came in sight I might know that all was well, and the letter had been posted safely. He looked somewhat exhausted when he reached the house, for the post-office was a long way off, and to wave a handkerchief steadily for twenty minutes is in itself a tiring exercise, but I learnt in time that Matthew never spared himself in the service of others.

END OF VOL. I.